THE EDGE OF THE AGE

WRAK-AYYA: THE AGE OF SHADOWS BOOK SEVEN

LEIGH ROBERTS

DRAGON WINGS PRESS

CONTENTS

Editing by Joy Sephton http://www.justemagine.biz
Cover design by Cherie Fox http://www.cheriefox.com

Sexual activities or events in this book are intended for adults.

ISBN: 978-1-951528-02-7 (ebook)
ISBN: 978-1-951528-15-7 (paperback)

CHAPTER 1

It was not long since the Leader, Khon'Tor, had granted his son, Akar'Tor permission to stay at High Rocks. This was on the advice of Kurak'Kahn, the High Council Overseer, who had reminded him that the most dangerous enemy is the one you cannot see coming. It seemed wise to keep the young upstart in clear view. At Khon'Tor's direction, the community leaders of the High Rocks had lined up an array of essential basic training for Akar'Tor, very little of which was likely to meet with his approval.

Akar'Tor looked up from his assignment—helping the females in the food preparation area. His ego stung from being relegated to what he considered menial tasks, and even worse, *female* tasks. He had come to Kthama to lead, not to be belittled by his father, Khon'Tor. He also hated to admit it, but he missed his mother, and Haan—the male who had helped raise him, and whom he still considered his real father. Even though Kayerm was nowhere as spacious or accommodating as Kthama and he would never truly fit in there with the Sarnonn, it was still home.

At least Adia, the Healer, is kind to me. She and her Waschini offspring, Oh'Dar, have been all along, though he is no longer here. But I do not like her mate, the High Protector, Acaraho. When I am Leader of the High Rocks, he will be one of the first to go.

As he worked, Akar'Tor scanned the common area for Khon'Tor, or Tehya, the Leader's mate. He made a point of avoiding Tehya as much as possible after being warned away by Khon'Tor, whom he now made a point of studying instead. But he still risked a fleeting glance at Tehya if he calculated that no one would notice.

He was always baffled when watching Khon'Tor speak with the other males. *What makes him so powerful? Why do people follow him? I see nothing special. He is as my mother said—arrogant, proud. I do not see why the females' eyes follow him so. Or what that beautiful Tehya sees in him.*

His thoughts wandered back to Tehya. Her soft, almost golden hair, her eyes the color of deep amber —nowhere as dark as nearly everyone else's. He wanted to be alone with her, to lay her down and press himself up against her as he had seen the adults at Kayerm do. He wanted to explore what was under the flowing wrappings she always wore; he wanted to make her moan as he had heard other females do when their males were on them.

Mapiya scolded him as another piece of wild apple skidded off the stone slab and hit the floor. "Pay attention, Akar'Tor. You are making a mess." Her slicing Handspeak movements matched the sharp tone in her voice.

Akar'Tor glared at her and muttered under his breath, "This is *krellshar*."

Adia had given everyone who would be working with him enough advice on how to understand his speech that they could follow most of what he was saying. But, advice or not, there was no doubt in Mapiya's mind as to what he had just said.

"Use that language again, offspring, and see what happens. I do not care who you think you are. You *will* act respectfully around the rest of us," she shot back.

Now she will probably go running to Khon'Tor! All these females need a lesson. Wait until I am Leader and see what happens, you old female, thought Akar'Tor as he went back to cutting up the foodstuffs in front of him.

Acaraho sat watching the young male from across the room, his mate, Adia, seated at his side.

"Are you thinking what I am thinking, Acaraho?" she asked.

"That he is going to be nothing but trouble? Yes," he replied.

"And just when I thought we had hit a lull. We are only now getting over losing our young females in the Ashwea Awhidi, and the impact of the sickness. And we have also just learned how much we did *not* know about our own history. Everything is up in the air—the whole incident with Haan and Hakani, and now Akar'Tor coming here. I long for the boring days."

"And just when *were* the boring days, Healer? Please remind me," laughed Acaraho.

She smiled back at him and—under the table—curled the toes of one foot around his.

"How long before Akar'Tor breaks?" she pondered aloud.

"He is highly-strung like his mother and strong-willed like his father. It is a toss-up, but considering the volatile relationship between him and Khon'Tor, I vote for sooner rather than later."

"I do feel a little sorry for him. His situation is not that different from Oh'Dar's. He does not belong here, and he does not belong among the Sarnonn," Adia said softly, watching Akar'Tor cleaning vegetables with the sourest of expressions. "It still always takes me by surprise that he looks so similar to Khon'Tor; even the silver streaks of hair running through their heads are the same."

"The difference is, despite all the warnings about how terrible the Waschini are, Oh'Dar has a sweet and helpful demeanor. No one could ever say that of Akar'Tor," replied Acaraho.

He is right, and I know that things between him and Khon'Tor will come to a head. But I wish it could be otherwise. I am tired of turmoil. And I hope to raise our offspring, whenever they come, in peace and calm, rather than this upheaval.

Adia and Acaraho were anxiously waiting for her to be seeded. Unlike most of the other males at Kthama, Acaraho had never come down with the sickness, so there was no reason to believe he could not father offspring. And though they had been conceived against Second Law, Adia already had two offspring—Nimida and Nootau—so her fertility was not in question. Still, the weeks and months had ticked by with no results.

Acaraho reached under the table and squeezed Adia's hand. "Want to try again tonight?" he asked.

"You have to ask? Anywhere, anytime; you should know that by now, Commander," and she looked him up and down with hooded lids.

Despite her attempt at levity, Acaraho noticed the sadness in her eyes.

"Do not worry, Saraste'. It will happen when the time is right," he reassured her.

Urilla Wuti, Adia, and Nadiwani were working in the Healer's Quarters, passing the morning together, though the Helper seemed slightly distracted. Kweeuu lay under the work table, hoping that something interesting would make it down to the floor. He was fully grown but still acted like a playful cub in many ways.

He also now followed Tehya every chance he got —partly because he loved the Leader's mate, but also reinforced by Oh'Dar's last order to protect her. Today he was with Nadiwani as Tehya had tasks to attend to that did not lend themselves to having a furry sidekick.

Urilla Wuti had stayed on after the High Council disbanded. She knew Tehya found her presence helpful, but the older Healer and Adia also had more work to do developing Adia's special Healer abilities. Urilla Wuti's duties back home were being covered by her niece, Iella, who had been apprenticing as Healer for some time. Iella also had the help of Urilla Wuti's midwives, and if anything urgent required the Healer's return, Urilla Wuti would sense it through the Connection.

Adia had experienced serious trouble when trying to disconnect from Haan after making a Connection with him, and knowing that he would be returning before too long, Urilla Wuti wanted to work with Adia on strengthening her boundaries. However, even after all this time working with the Connection, Urilla Wuti freely admitted she did not know everything.

Until now, she and Adia had not told Nadiwani

about the Connection. Nadiwani was not a Healer, though she did possess a higher seventh sense than the other females. On the chance that she might be able to develop the skill, Urilla Wuti wanted to try.

She turned to Nadiwani. "Adia and I would like to talk to you about something important."

"Of course, what is it?"

Once they were settled in a circle, Adia started.

"When Urilla Wuti first came to help me when I was with offspring, she talked to me about some special talents that, with proper training, certain Healers can develop. She and I have been working on these abilities for years now. Only a small circle knows of them. We thought you should be included in that circle," and she looked across at Urilla Wuti, who took over.

"Not everyone can develop these gifts, but for those who can, I believe they will, at some point, become crucial for the People as we navigate the challenges ahead. I do not know why some can do it, and some cannot; there does not seem to be a pattern. It may have a hereditary component, but we do not know because Healers were always forbidden to reproduce. Now that the restriction has been lifted by the High Council, over time, we should be able to tell. If it can be hereditary, perhaps Nimida will in time develop a higher seventh sense—though at the moment I do not detect it, and from experience, it should have become evident by now."

Adia was sorry to hear that, but she had to

concur; she had also not picked up any special seventh sense in her daughter. But the daughter of Urilla Wuti's brother, Iella, was now apprenticing under Urilla Wuti—so perhaps it was handed down in some cases.

She spoke now. "When it was time to induce Hakani's labor, I was terribly worried about Haan's reaction if she or the offspring did not survive. I wanted to convince him that we were doing everything we could to save them both. I did not feel I could make Haan understand by speaking to him, so I opened between us what is called a Connection. Afterward, I found I could understand his speech far better. And then, of course, Oh'Dar came up with the idea of combining Handspeak with speaking, and that helped everyone else.

"We are learning from Haan that many of the beliefs we have about our history are wrong. As stories are passed down, they are distorted. Having only a small circle know the truth has turned out to be to our detriment. So we want to try to bring you into this circle, and we are urging the Healers of the other communities to do the same," Adia continued.

Nadiwani listened silently, holding her questions for now.

"A Connection can be opened with anyone," continued Urilla Wuti, "but only someone with the ability can instigate it. I do have to warn you that connecting with another person is extremely intimate. With your permission, Nadiwani, I would like to open a Connection with you. There are many levels, and I will only join with you at the first one, which will preserve the largest majority of your privacy. We will experience each other's primary memories at a level that can only be demonstrated. Are you willing to join me in this way?"

"Yes, I am honored to be included, and though I may not be able to create it myself, I want to know about this," she answered.

"I know you have a higher seventh sense than most, even though it is not developed to the level needed by a Healer. And who am I to say who can learn to do this? Even after all these years, I am still learning too," said Urilla Wuti.

With that, she turned to face Nadiwani and took both her hands.

"Close your eyes and accept my invitation," the older Healer said. Urilla Wuti's abilities had developed, and she was becoming more adept at keeping the first level shallow. When they separated, Nadiwani would not have as long a recovery period as Adia had required in the past.

Within a moment, the window that was the Connection opened into Nadiwani's mind. She felt herself merge with Urilla Wuti, and their experiences converged.

Nadiwani was no longer herself. She experienced the joys and burdens of Urilla Wuti's life, unbearable grief at her brother's passing, and the pain of not being able to save him. She was filled with Urilla

Wuti's bittersweet joy when, a while later, she held his newborn daughter in her arms for the first time. She felt the history between Urilla Wuti and Tehya, Khon'Tor's mate, and a myriad of other memories and experiences now became part of her own.

After a few moments, Urilla Wuti broke the Connection, and Nadiwani felt them pull apart. Her head was fuzzy, and she sat with her eyes closed for a few moments as she separated into one person again. Finally, she looked up.

"I do not know what to say. I had no idea that was even possible. I can see why this could be a powerful tool," she said.

"So you understand why this ability is not shared openly? Like other areas of our Healer's knowledge, some of it is shrouded in secrecy for the greater good," said Urilla Wuti.

Though she had not controlled the Connection, Nadiwani was still feeling the effects. "I think I need to lie down," she said.

Adia got up and helped her over to the sleeping mat in the corner. "What you are feeling is a natural effect of making a Connection. It will pass," she said as she placed a covering over the Helper. "We will leave you alone for a while," she added.

Kweeuu came over and curled up against the Helper's back, sensing that she needed his comfort. Nadiwani reached back and petted him, then closed her eyes.

Adia and Urilla Wuti left quietly. Adia knew that Nadiwani's world had now changed forever. She wondered how much information had been shared between them.

"Do you think there is a possibility that Nadiwani could develop these abilities?" she asked Urilla Wuti as they walked.

"I truly do not know. There was a time when, with confidence, I would have said no. But now I am not as sure of myself as I was."

"Yes. Haan's information has rocked our foundations," said Adia. "I hope it will be a while before he comes back. As it is, we have enough to deal with given what he has told us already."

Awan beckoned as he spoke, "Come with me, son."

First Guard Awan came to collect Akar'Tor from where he was working with Mapiya.

Akar'Tor threw down the cutting blade he had been using. Mapiya frowned as it skidded across the work surface.

"Where are we going?"

"To your next lesson."

Once outside, Awan led Akar'Tor down to the area by the Great River. With no cloud cover, the hot summer sun beat down mercilessly. Along the river banks, a group of females stood at the shallow river's edge with hunting spears in hand.

Good. This is better. No doubt it will be my job to organize these females and make sure they do not slack off.

Awan led Akar'Tor up to one of them.

"This is Donoma. She will tell you what to do," and Awan walked away, leaving Akar'Tor with his mouth hanging open. Once partway up the hillside, the guard turned back to watch the exchange.

Donoma turned to Akar'Tor. "You must have been spearfishing before?" she asked.

"Yes, *of course*," he answered curtly.

"There is your station over there. As we catch them, your job is to clean them. Do you know how to do that?"

Akar'Tor sneered. "That is females' work."

"Well, today it is *your* work," said Donoma, and she also turned and walked away.

Donoma was not comfortable being curt like this to anyone, but she was under strict direction from Khon'Tor to give Akar'Tor no quarter—as were all those to whom the young male had been assigned for work duty.

The long grasses bent under his feet as Akar'Tor stomped off in a huff.

Confident that this would be the extent of his

acting out, Awan turned back to Kthama to report to Khon'Tor.

"How is it going?" asked the Leader as Awan approached.

"As you expected, Adik'Tar. I have to hand it to Donoma; she is playing her part well."

"As is Mapiya from what I have heard."

"In my opinion, he will be a hard one to crack."

"Like the trees in the winter storm—he will either bend, or he will break. He is not fit to join our community as he is. If he does not learn some humility and respect, I will ban him from Kthama," was Khon'Tor's dry response. "Does Donoma know to release Akar for the day when she is finished with him?"

"Yes, Khon'Tor."

"Very well."

By early afternoon, Akar'Tor reeked of fish guts and sweat. His eyes stung from the beads of perspiration that had run down his forehead. Scales were stuck all over his body hair. He had not eaten, and he had not relieved himself for some time with the females around. None of this improved his attitude.

Finally, Donoma dismissed the work crew and approached Akar'Tor.

"Please take the cleaned fish up to the females in the work preparation area. They will know what to do with them. Then come back and clean up the area. You can push the leavings into the river."

Akar'Tor gritted his teeth, "And *then what*?"

"Khon'Tor said that you are done for the day after you clean up here. Report back to Mapiya in the morning after first light. But before you go back to Kthama, I suggest you take a dip in the Great River and dry out. You stink something awful."

Donoma turned quickly to hide her face and walked away briskly. *I know this is for his benefit. I hope it works, but he looks pretty angry. I think I should let Khon'Tor know how it went.*

Donoma found the leader in a meeting room with Acaraho, Awan, and Mapiya.

"Excuse me; may I give you an update on Akar'-Tor's work today," she said, peeking her head into the room.

Khon'Tor motioned her in.

"We just finished. He should be bringing the cleaned fish up shortly. I told him to push the leavings into the river and then clean up before returning to Kthama. He smells terrible."

Acaraho lowered his head to suppress a smile.

"Does he know he has the rest of the day off?"

"Yes, I told him. Also, I said he must report to Mapiya at first light. It was hard to be curt with him; it is not in my nature. But I do understand, Adik'Tar, that it is for his own good. He truly is an insolent one, and he has a mouth on him, that is for sure!" she added.

"Thank you, Donoma. You did well," answered Khon'Tor, and he excused her.

"Awan, make sure Akar'Tor's whereabouts are known at all times. And that he never approaches Tehya or the Leader's Quarters," said Acaraho. "And remind all the watchers and the other guards."

"It has already been taken care of, Commander."

Acaraho nodded and turned to Khon'Tor. "What is on his schedule for tomorrow?"

"After he finishes with helping Mapiya again, I will be training him in some defensive fight techniques."

"That will be more to his liking."

"Not if it goes as I have planned," said Khon'Tor, then added, "thank you, everyone. That is all for now."

Awan and Mapiya left, leaving Acaraho and Khon'Tor alone in the room.

"Do you not think you are baiting him too much?" asked Acaraho.

"Perhaps, if I thought there was any chance of his truly fitting in. But the sooner he breaks, the sooner he will be out of here—one way or the other."

"Where will you be training him?"

"Down in the valley. Are you concerned I cannot handle him?"

"Not for a moment," said Acaraho. "Akar'Tor is younger, perhaps has faster reflexes, but he is not experienced, and he has problems controlling his emotions. I thought Tehya would prefer you had someone with you."

Khon'Tor thought about that for a moment. *I do not want her to worry, and no doubt she will get wind of this at some point, either before or after. The other guards will be there, but I know she trusts Acaraho the most.* "I bow to your judgment. It will be during the morning, and I will make sure you are notified."

The next day, Akar'Tor reported to Mapiya. He had spent the previous afternoon drying out from his bath in the Great River and sulking in his quarters. He hated that there were always guards with him seeing his continual humiliation, even if in the distance.

"I do not need you this morning, but Khon'Tor is waiting for you at the Great Entrance. I suggest you go there directly," said Mapiya.

Akar'Tor did so to find not only Khon'Tor but also Acaraho waiting there for him.

"I was asked to come here to find you," he said.

"I believe the accurate statement is that you were *told* to come here," said Khon'Tor. "Come with us."

"Where are we going?" he asked.

"You will find out when we get there," and Khon'Tor walked away with Acaraho in the direction of the valley, the two guards following behind their charge.

When they reached the clearing—which had been prepared ahead of time and was free of rocks, sticks, and other debris—Khon'Tor explained why they were there.

"You wish to learn the ways of the People. Though we are not aggressive, there will always be times when you must defend yourself. Today we will be working on your fighting skills."

Akar'Tor scoffed to himself. *Quat! This will not take long. He is old, and I will have him on the ground in moments.*

"Before I can teach you, I must see what you already know. When you are ready—" said Khon'Tor.

Akar'Tor shook his head, "Remember, you asked for it!" He charged Khon'Tor head-on.

Khon'Tor waited, and just as Akar'Tor was about to tackle him, turned out of the way. Using Akar'Tor's momentum, the Leader gave him a push that sent him sailing past and crashing into the ground.

Akar'Tor shook himself off and took a moment to get his bearings. He stood, his face screwed up while he picked small stones out of his palms and brushed off his arms.

"I dare you to try that again!" shouted the young male, and he made another mad dash straight at Khon'Tor, with the same results.

Acaraho watched from the sidelines.

Akar'Tor's anger was evident. He changed his approach, arms out, crouched, circling Khon'Tor looking for an advantage, a snarl curling his lips.

Khon'Tor stood still, erect, arms relaxed at his side, his eyes calmly following Akar'Tor, waiting for the tell that he was making a move. He was leaving himself fully open for an attack.

His father's nonchalant, unguarded posture enraged Akar'Tor all that much more. Tired of waiting, he again made the first move.

The distance between the two gave Khon'Tor more than enough time to effect a defense. As Akar'Tor came at him, the Leader timed it perfectly, twisting to catch the young male directly in the chest with a raised hip, knocking him out of breath to the ground.

Akar'Tor gasped, clutching his chest as he tried to force air back into his emptied lungs.

Khon'Tor waited a few moments for him to recover, then walked over and extended his arm to help him up.

Akar'Tor angrily swatted his father's hand out of the way and tried, on his own, to bring himself up on one knee, still struggling for air.

Khon'Tor turned and walked a few feet back toward Kthama, then turned and said, "Count yourself lucky, Akar. I could just have easily broken your ribs. I think our lesson is over for this morning. Once you recover, return to your quarters for the balance of the day. Do not leave except to attend the evening meal."

With that, Khon'Tor and Acaraho headed back home, leaving Akar'Tor and his guards in the valley. When they were well out of earshot, Acaraho said,

"He seems to know nothing about fighting,"

"It makes sense when you think about it. The Sarnonn have no viable enemies. And they are not aggressive. Add their size to that, and they have no need of technique," said Khon'Tor.

"I expect he learned nothing useful," said Acaraho.

"Unfortunately, I am afraid you are wrong. He learned that he will never beat me in hand-to-hand combat. That means, if he wants to best me, he will have to find a way other than to take me head-on. And, unfortunately, his mother was a master at being devious."

Khon'Tor stopped to face Acaraho. "I want to believe that this is just a young buck testing his mettle against the lead stag, but there is more to it. He hates me, and the feeling is mutual. But I have only made it worse with my behavior. I did not end the training because he needed a break—I ended it because I needed one. I feared what I would do to him if it continued. Had I brought my knee up instead of using my hip, I could easily have killed him."

Acaraho listened silently before speaking.

"I agree. We all need to be vigilant with Akar'Tor, and especially you. I do believe he hates you—most likely from stories Hakani has told, passing her bitterness on to him. We cannot risk underestimating him, and the sooner he is gone from Kthama, the better off we will all be."

And the two giants silently made the rest of their way up the trail back to Kthama.

Khon'Tor still carried the tension of the day when he retired, nodding to the two guards in the corridor that lead to his quarters. He entered quietly, expecting Tehya to be asleep as she always had been lately.

She was a tiny curve under the covers of their sleeping mat. He eased himself in next to her, pulling her delicate frame over against his. She murmured and instinctively threw an arm and a leg over him, enjoying the added warmth he brought.

His eyes wandered over her features as she slept. Her nearly-honey-gold hair lay splayed in all directions on the mat. Her skin glowed. Her eyelids fluttered as if she were dreaming. He brushed a piece of hair from her forehead and remembered the taste of her soft lips.

His pulse quickened as she cuddled closer. He could not help his response; just looking at her drove him wild. He loosened the front of her nighttime wrapping and watched her breasts rise and fall with her soft breathing. Not being able to help himself, he teased one of the soft tips, and she moaned in her sleep. He ran his hand down over the small of her back and pressed her hips tighter into him. She slowly opened her eyes and smiled. He leaned down, and she welcomed his lips on hers. In the next moment, she was aroused enough to roll over on top of him, the front of her wrapping now fully open. Her legs straddled him, and shifting, she took him into herself, moving over him in the most pleasurable way.

Khon'Tor smiled at the surprise. *This is adventurous for her,* he thought. He placed his hands on her hips but let her move as she wished, his turn to surrender to her. She closed her eyes as she rode him, each movement bringing them both delicious waves of pleasure.

As Tehya's rhythm increased, Khon'Tor could finally take it no more, and in one move, rolled her over onto her back and took control. Each stroke brought sounds of pleasure from her lips, and he increased the intensity, answering the pressure of her hands as they pulled him farther into her. As soon as he could tell she was cresting, he let go and lost himself as he emptied all he had into her. His entire body stiffened in release as he pressed himself as deep within her as he dared. After a while, he rolled onto his back and pulled her close to him, her head resting in the crook of his shoulder.

He looked down to see tears streaming down Tehya's cheeks. "What's wrong? Please tell me!" And he gently brushed them away with his thumb. "*Did I hurt you?*"

"I love you so much, Adoeete. I never knew I could care this much about anyone."

He closed his eyes and held her close. "As I love you, Tehya. Nothing but you matters to me anymore. You are all I want in the whole of Etera," he said.

"There is no other?" she asked.

"There will never be another," he assured her.

"But could there not be room in your heart for one more?" she asked.

He looked at her frowning, totally confused. *Surely she was not suggesting—* "No, never. Not possible. *What are you talking about?*" he asked as he propped himself up on his other elbow to look at her squarely.

"I just thought perhaps there might be room in your heart for one more. Perhaps, just a *small one?*" She smiled now, clearly teasing him.

"Tehya—"

"Yes, Adoeete. Your relentless bedding of me has proved successful, and your seed has taken root. I am carrying your offspring!"

Khon'Tor laughed out loud and dragged her up into his arms, cradling her gently. He wanted to shout to the world, but the moment was too tender. He pulled her back and looked at her.

"Should I not have— But you started it—" he stammered.

"Technically *you* started it, I was sleeping innocently," kidded Tehya. "And you finished it. I just helped a little in the middle."

Khon'Tor chuckled then circled his arms around her again.

"How far along are you now?" he asked.

"About five months. I wanted to be sure before I said anything. I am surprised you have not noticed."

Remembered pain rushed anew over Khon'Tor. *Five months and she is hardly showing. I did not even notice it. That is when she lost the first one, but she was very sick and had lost so much weight from not eating. And if she is five months along, then she was seeded right after she lost the first one—before I got sick.*

Worried that this might still be the only offspring he could seed, he pushed the thought away quickly so as not to ruin her joy.

"I did think you were getting a little plump, now that you mention it," he lied.

"What!" she exclaimed. And as she was wont to do, she pounded his chest playfully. Seeing the look in his eyes that her fake protestations always incited, she added, "Oh, alright. One more time."

"No. No. I do not want to take any chances."

"It is alright, Adoeete. I asked Adia. It is fine for a few more months yet."

"The Healer knows you are with offspring? Who else? *I do all the work, and I am the last to know*?"

"Nobody else," she chuckled. "Adia only knows because I wanted to be sure. She has told no one, I promise. But whenever you want to announce it, we can."

"Let it be our secret a while longer, Tehya. I want to cherish this time between us."

He laid her back down and held her close.

"Did Adia have any concerns? Because of how small you are?" He could not help but think of Hakani and Haan and the size difference between them and how Haan's offspring could not be carried to term without the risk of killing Hakani.

"I asked her that. She said we would watch carefully. But my ancestors are also small. The offspring might take more after my side," she replied.

"You must promise to tell me everything. I will not risk you, Tehya. Not even for—"

"Hush. It will be fine. I will be mindful, I promise."

Khon'Tor looked over at his Leader's Staff in its place in the corner, remembering the moments before Adia's decision at the High Council—when he thought he would be ruined and his staff publicly broken and burned, ending the 'Tor line in disgrace and shame.

He closed his eyes and thanked the Great Spirit for his many blessings, for the forgiveness that had given him this second chance at love, at happiness, and another opportunity to be the great Khon'Tor, Leader of the People of the High Rocks.

Perhaps one day, I will have a son who can carry on the 'Tor line. But not even that is worth risking Tehya's life. I trust what she is telling me is true, but I will still also talk to the Healer.

CHAPTER 2

Akar'Tor's training continued. Over the next several weeks, Khon'Tor kept him busy with a line-up of tasks that involved helping in various areas around Kthama. Khon'Tor kept his distance, getting regular updates from Mapiya, Awan, Acaraho, and Donoma.

"So, where are we now?" the Leader asked.

"So far he has helped in the meal preparation area, cleaned fish caught from the river, been bested by you in hand-to-hand combat, learned rudimentary weaving techniques with Mapiya, gathered new bedding material for the storeroom, helped Tar clean the Gonaii, restacked the supply storerooms under Mapiya's direction, and today is out gathering Goldenseal with Nadiwani and the little ones."

"Is it that time of year again?" remarked Khon'-Tor. "How has his behavior been?"

"A lot of dirty looks, some immature kicking over

of a basket of live fish, which only resulted in more work—chasing them as they flopped around loose. And a great deal of swearing under his breath. The Sarnonn must curse a lot. Some of those words I remember only hearing once before—when I was an offspring and my father dropped a hammer rock on his toes," said Mapiya.

They chuckled despite themselves. The females virtually never used bad language and males rarely in front of the females or offspring.

"Has anyone else anything to report?"

"He is followed everywhere, of course," shared Awan. "I have seen him leave Kthama at night and go down into the valley. Mapiya mentioned his foul language, well, he walks around swearing and usually tosses some rocks and boulders before returning. Letting off steam no doubt; he is strong, Khon'Tor,"

"I am aware; thank you for the reminder. Any sign of him watching Tehya or approaching her, or our quarters?"

"No, Adik'Tar. Trust us, we would have told you if there had been, even if we were *not* under orders. Everyone loves Tehya. They would be destroyed if any harm came to her. He seems to make a point of not looking at her—but he does spend a fair amount of time watching you, for whatever reason."

Khon'Tor nodded. Tehya was so different from Hakani. Due to her sour personality, the community had never taken to his first mate.

"Thank you, everyone. Acaraho, may I have a word with you alone?"

The others filed out.

"Has Adia told you that Tehya is with offspring?" asked Khon'Tor.

"No, she has not. Congratulations! How far along is she?"

"Probably six months now. She has been wearing looser wrappings, and some will notice soon. I know I should make an announcement—"

"But you do not want to call attention to her with Akar'Tor here—" finished Acaraho.

"Exactly."

Silence.

"I do not see a way around it, Adik'Tar."

Khon'Tor never failed to notice when Acaraho addressed him as Adik'Tar, or Adoeete, great Leader. There was a time when he would have taken that as a veiled insult. But their relationship had changed, and now Khon'Tor was fairly sure he could receive it as a show of respect. He ran his hand through his silver crest.

"We will do everything we can to protect her. Why do you think he would harm her?" asked Acaraho. Though he had his theories, he wanted to hear Khon'Tor's.

"Because that is what Hakani would do. There is only one way to destroy me—through hurting Tehya."

While they were still talking, Akule came in with a message.

"Khon'Tor, we have received word from the High Council that many of the other communities now have the sickness."

"Before we discuss this, go and find Adia and Nadiwani and bring them here to us," said Khon'Tor.

In a few minutes, the watcher returned with the females.

"Right, Akule, what is the message?" asked Khon'Tor.

"All the communities up the Mother Stream are sending reports that they have the sickness. I have not heard from those farther out."

Adia and Nadiwani looked at each other.

"We must still have been contagious," sighed Acaraho.

"Possibly, but I think we would have seen resurgence here first. Or perhaps some immunity develops as people recover, yet somehow they can still make others sick," Adia added.

"We have no way of knowing which it is. But this makes our situation more urgent," said Khon'Tor.

"Is there any word about which of the High Council members already has it? And are they asking for help?"Acaraho asked Akule.

"So far, Lesharo'Mok and Kurak'Kahn are the only ones specifically mentioned. Both are doing well, though, and expected to recover fully. There was no request for assistance."

"This will delay our meeting again. I know the Overseer wanted to be here when Haan returned to open Kthama Minor. Perhaps we should get word to Haan that there may be a delay," said Acaraho.

Khon'Tor nodded. "We do not know when he was planning on returning; he said he had to prepare. See if you can get word to him. And let us hope that whatever secrets are buried in Kthama Minor also give up some answers."

Tehya stood looking down at her growing belly, wondering if others could tell. She was running out of larger garments and would soon need to ask someone for a loan. So far, Khon'Tor had not made an announcement, though she had no idea if this was unusual or not.

She suddenly felt someone watching her and turned to see her mate in the doorway.

"Adoeete, I did not hear your approach," she exclaimed. "Look how big I am getting," and she turned to show him her profile.

"Pretty soon, I will no longer be able to carry you," he teased.

She pretended to ignore him. "Have you eaten yet? I am famished."

"I am pleased to hear you have an appetite," said Khon'Tor. "Shall I have something brought here?"

"If you do not mind, I would like to eat with

everyone else tonight. I can wear something bulky if you still are not prepared for others to know," she offered.

"Oh, no, it is time we make an official announcement. It is just—"

"Is it Akar'Tor? I know; you do not have to tell me, but he never even looks at me anymore. If anything, he seems to be intentionally avoiding me," she said.

"I will feel better once he is gone. But it is not fair on you—you deserve to celebrate your joy with the other females. I promise, tomorrow I will call a general assembly and make the announcement. Now, let us get you something to eat before you vanish before my eyes," he said.

"Make up your mind, Adoeete. Either I am too big for you to carry, or I am wasting away—it cannot be both!"

Khon'Tor went over, stooped down, wrapped his muscular arms around her hips, and grunted—pretending he could hardly lift her—and they both laughed.

He waited while she changed her wrappings and was pleased to see she had put on the necklace he had designed for her. Kweeuu came off his sleeping mat and trotted happily behind them to the Great Chamber.

Akar'Tor saw his father and Tehya enter the general eating area and make their way to the table they usually shared with Adia and Acaraho. He kept his eyes on Khon'Tor, only daring to steal a glance at Tehya when he was confident he would not be caught.

Acaraho had positioned himself where he could keep an eye on the young male and watched as Akar'Tor's eyes followed the couple.

Once Tehya was seated, Khon'Tor excused himself and went to speak with Adia, who was involved with a group of females at another table.

"Healer. A moment?" he asked.

Adia excused herself and followed Khon'Tor out of earshot.

"As you know, Tehya is seeded. I am going to announce it tomorrow. I need to hear from you that she is not at any risk," he said.

"I know how much this means to you both, and I know how much *she* means to you. Yes, she did lose the offspring before, but she was very ill and had lost weight she could not afford to lose. Even you can see she is gaining weight nicely now," Adia explained.

"But Hakani and Haan—the size—"

"It is true; she is small, one of the smallest of the People I have ever seen. And you are one of the biggest, but so far, I do not see a problem. Remember that Urilla Wuti is also here. If I had any concerns, I would have already come to you," Adia assured him.

Khon'Tor sighed and looked back over at Tehya, who was laughing with the others at their table.

Adia put her hand on Khon'Tor's arm to bring his attention back. The Leader looked briefly down at her touch. In his recollection, other than the night when he had attacked her, and the two times she had slapped him hard across his face, she had never touched him.

"Khon'Tor, we all love Tehya, and we know how much you do. I promise we will not let anything happen to her or the offspring,"

"I have never heard you make a promise like that. It gives me peace; thank you."

Khon'Tor returned to join his mate, straddling the bench and cradling her between his thighs, as usual deliberately and publicly claiming her as his. He noticed that someone had brought her food and was pleased to see her eating.

Then he froze.

He shot his hand out in front of Tehya and slammed it down on top of her meal, sending food-stuffs flying everywhere. Shocked, she and the others looked over at him wide-eyed.

"*Who brought this? Who made this?*" he demanded.

Tehya blurted out, "Mapiya! She said she made it for me herself!"

Acaraho nodded agreement, and Khon'Tor removed his hand, shaking remnants of food to the floor, of which Kweeuu happily made short work.

Tehya looked at what was left of her food, smashed around on the table in front of her.

Acaraho turned and signed to Mapiya, who was already on her way over, having heard the commotion.

"What is it? Is something wrong?" Mapiya asked.

Looking down at the mess in front of Tehya, she joked, "I take it that the food was not to your liking?" It broke the tension, and everyone laughed.

"No, he just thinks I am getting fat," said Tehya, and they all laughed again.

"I—overreacted," said Khon'Tor.

"I will bring a fresh serving," smiled Mapiya.

Tehya looked over at her mate, concern creasing her brow. *He is not himself lately. I am sure it is about my being with offspring and everything else going on. Maybe I should stay in our quarters until things settle down.*

Khon'Tor collected himself. "Acaraho, call a general assembly for the morning. I have an announcement."

Then, fleetingly, Tehya saw something she had never expected to see flash across Khon'Tor's face. Something that looked very much like fear.

Hakani held their daughter while Haan rearranged the sleeping mats. Kalli had started crawling now and was into everything. Hakani appreciated the help the other females gave her, and especially her friend Haaka, who would often look after Kalli when Hakani needed a break.

Once everything was straightened up, they settled down for the night. The warm light from the entrance fire was a welcoming glow around the edges of the hide curtain. Facing Haan, Hakani curled around little Kalli, who was content to be cuddled safely against her mother.

Just before sleep was the hardest time for Hakani. In the quiet at the end of the day, her thoughts would go to Akar'Tor, wishing he would come home. She ached to know what was going on. In her fantasies, she imagined him insinuating himself into the community of the High Rocks and eventually becoming the Leader, which would allow her to return. But in her more lucid moments, she was afraid of losing him. Life was hard at Kayerm, and the thought of never seeing him again made living there just that much more unbearable, even with little Kalli to raise.

"Are you asleep?" she asked.

"No."

"I cannot help worrying about Akar," she said quietly.

Haan answered softly. "Akar has to find his own way. This is not a problem that either of us can solve for him."

"I do not know if I can stand to wait. Not knowing what is going on— It is too hard, Haan. I know in my gut that at some point, Khon'Tor and Akar will go head-to-head."

"Khon'Tor would not harm him, though he will hopefully teach Akar a much-needed lesson or two. Try to stand it a while longer, Hakani; I will have to return to Kthama before too long. But if it gets unbearable, we can go together before then—just you and I—to visit him. But it would have to be brief."

"Are you sure?" Hakani propped her self up on one elbow, and sudden tears rolled down her face, confusing her. "Thank you, Haan. *Thank you*."

She lay back down, cuddled Kalli closer, and felt that, finally, she would fall asleep.

Near the end of the first meal, the Call to Assembly Horn sounded, though almost everyone was already seated. Mapiya and the others had already spread the word that Khon'Tor would be addressing them all that morning.

Khon'Tor looked out over the crowd, spotting the thorn in his side, Akar'Tor, standing at the back near the entrance. Not far from him was one of the two guards assigned to follow his every move.

The Leader took Tehya's hand and led her to the front. Silence fell across the group as they realized he was carrying the Leader's Staff. He raised his left hand. "It has been a few weeks since I last addressed you. I know the past year has been trying for us all. We have lost many whom we loved through the sickness that ravaged our community, and though it was a time of celebration, many of our maidens left because of the Ashwea Awhidi. But today I come to give you news that I hope will lift your spirits."

Khon'Tor stopped and looked over at his mate as she stood next to him. He raised her hand in his. "Tehya is with offspring."

The crowd broke out in smiles and cheers. Khon'Tor could not help but contrast it with the comparatively forced reaction when he had stood here many years ago and told them Hakani was seeded. *Tehya is genuinely beloved, as Adia has said.*

After a moment, he continued, "I do not have to tell you how much happiness this brings me. Please celebrate with us as this is a truly joyous occasion."

Khon'Tor stood a moment to let Tehya absorb the welcoming and happy smiles across the sea of faces. Then he led her from the platform, taking a fleeting glance at Akar'Tor in the back as they stepped down.

The look on Akar'Tor's face was anything but celebratory.

That PetaQ, thought Akar'Tor.

The Sarnonn did not have the same expectations of privacy in mating as did the People, though the People did tolerate public displays of flirting.

Back at Kayerm, he had walked in on others mating, and it sickened him to think of Khon'Tor doing that to Tehya. *It is disgusting. That should be my seed growing in her, not his. He is old and used up, and she would be far better off with someone her age. If only I could talk to her, she would see that we belong together.*

Akar'Tor knew he had to get to Tehya, even for just a few minutes, and even if it had to be here, in public.

The couple was surrounded by well-wishers, though Khon'Tor was distracted. He was trying to keep an eye on Akar'Tor, who now stood just off to the side. The Leader steeled himself, suppressing his urge to take Tehya out of there, not wanting to cut short her enjoyment as the females showered warmth and sisterhood on her.

As Akar'Tor moved closer to them, Acaraho came over to intercept him. Standing in front of the young male, he put out his hand and commanded him to stop. Kweeuu growled from under the table where they had been eating earlier.

"You have no business here, son," Acaraho said.

"I am not your son, and my business here is *none of yours!*" he spat out. "I only want to congratulate my father and his mate."

Tehya and Khon'Tor stopped and turned toward

Akar'Tor. The Leader narrowed his eyes to slits and glared at the insolent male.

"I just want to talk to Tehya for a moment," said Akar'Tor.

"You can say what you want from here," said Acaraho, Akar'Tor now sandwiched between him in front and the guard behind. The High Protector wondered where the second guard was but dismissed it for the moment.

"Why are you all afraid of me? I must be very powerful for you to worry so about every move I make—guards always two steps behind me!" Akar'Tor sneered.

Khon'Tor stepped forward, with one arm pushing Tehya behind him. "Powerful? You are anything but powerful. What you are is immature. You have repeatedly proven you cannot control yourself or your emotions."

"You are afraid to let me be around her because you know I can take her from you," said Akar'Tor, puffing up his chest and standing as tall as he could. "There is nothing you can give her or do for her that I cannot do better. You need to step aside and let someone her age show her what a real male is!"

Within seconds, Khon'Tor had stepped around Akar'Tor and had him by the throat, lifting him off his feet despite their similar size, his face inches from his son's. Akar'Tor's hands clawed at the grip around his neck.

"You are running out of chances, Akar. If I even

see you looking at her again, I will *kill* you." With no more words said, Khon'Tor held Akar'Tor suspended before finally releasing him and tossing him hard onto the stone floor. The young male lay gasping for breath.

"Get him out of here," Acaraho ordered as the second guard finally showed up. They dragged Akar'Tor to his feet, just as Tehya stepped forward.

"No, wait!" she said.

She took a step forward to address Akar'Tor, who was now very firmly under the guards' control. She locked her eyes on his, and said with an unmistakable chill in her voice, "I do not know what is wrong with you. I have never given you a second thought, nor do I have any interest in you *whatsoever*. And the fact that you think for a moment you are any threat to Khon'Tor and me proves how confused you are."

She looked him up and down, frowning, "You may look like him, lucky for you, but that is where any resemblance ends. If you live to be four hundred, you will still never be a *sliver* as great as Khon'Tor is. You need to go back home to your mother and Haan. You had your chance, but you yourself have proven there is no place for you here—and there *never will be!*"

Tehya then turned her back to him and walked away, her skirted wrapping flipping behind her, leaving everyone with their mouths hanging open.

Khon'Tor looked at his son and smirked before going after her.

Followed by Kweeuu, Tehya made it around the corner out of sight and leaned against the wall, her legs shaking. Khon'Tor caught up with them in moments and whisked her up into his arms.

"Remind me never to cross you, my little sprite," he said as he carried her farther from the assembly area before setting her back down.

"Are you alright?" he asked after she stopped trembling.

"I hated to be mean to him, Khon'Tor. But he needed to hear it from me. Whatever fantasy he has going on in his head has to be squashed. Maybe the public humiliation will force him to give up and go home," she said.

He placed a finger under Tehya's chin and raised her face, leaning in and tenderly touching his lips to hers. She met his affection hungrily, wrapping her arms around his neck and pressing herself against him. He snaked his fingers through the hair at the back of Tehya's neck and ran his other hand down to the small of her back, pulling her in harder. Stopping to catch a breath, he exclaimed, "By the Spirit, Tehya, I have never wanted anyone as I want you. You keep me constantly on fire."

He closed his eyes to gain control of himself. "I have to stop. And you should get back to your fans. I am sure Acaraho has dispatched the guards with

Akar to confinement in his quarters by now," he added.

She ran her fingers over his lips and then smoothed the stray strands of his wild hair away from his temple. She leaned up on tiptoes to press her lips to his again.

"As you wish, Adoeete," she whispered in his ear.

Kweeuu had stood there the entire time, batting his huge fluffy tail up against Tehya.

Having seen everything that had just happened, Adia started to wonder if perhaps there was something wrong with Akar'Tor's mind.

After the guards had cleared him from the room, she turned to Nadiwani and Urilla Wuti. "He cannot believe that Tehya would have anything to do with him, can he? He is either out of touch with reality or incredibly egotistical. Or both. Perhaps he inherited the worst of each of them. I have heard Khon'Tor say Akar'Tor was conceived in hatred—could that affect an offspring? Or is it more likely that he has just been poisoned by Hakani?"

"I do not know. I believe that Hakani only came here because she was desperate. After all, she lived with Haan for all those years. Surely she did not nurse her bitterness all that time? " said Nadiwani.

"Some wounds appear healed, but once reopened, begin to fester," added Urilla Wuti.

The two guards took Akar'Tor back to his quarters and then assumed their posts. It was a tedious duty, and sometimes conversation was the only way to pass the time.

"He looks so much like Khon'Tor," said the first guard.

"I heard the Leader gave Akar'Tor his first lesson in fighting."

"What I would have given to see that. He also needs a good lesson in manners *and* respect. I do not see how he will ever fit in here, Kahrok."

"No. It is just a matter of time. I give Khon'Tor credit for allowing him a chance. I would have thrown the Soltark out long ago."

Acaraho came around the corner and addressed the second guard, "A word with you alone, Kahrok."

The guard followed Aracaho around the corner.

"You were not with Akar'Tor in the Great Chamber this morning."

"I am sorry, Commander. I have no excuse," he said. "It will not happen again, I promise."

"I will remove you from the rotation as soon as I select another," said Acaraho. "From now on, you will be assigned as a watcher."

"Because of *one* mistake, Commander?" Kahrock raised his voice and frowned hard.

"Of all the assignments, the protection of the Leader's mate is the highest priority. I cannot take a chance of another lapse. Return to your post for now, please."

Acaraho walked away, disappointed. It was the first time he remembered any of his guards letting him down, and this was a critical assignment. He did not know the cause but could not risk Akar'Tor ever again being monitored only partially. *I am sure Khon'Tor noticed it, though he said nothing. He trusts me to take care of it.*

🜨

Akar'Tor stomped around his room. *How could she say that to me? And in front of all the others. She must have been saying it for his benefit. I have to find a way to be alone with her, so she will admit that I am who she really wants!*

🜨

Tehya returned to the crowd of well-wishers.

Nadiwani was grinning from ear to ear. "Good for you, Tehya; I am glad you set him straight. I have never liked his interest in you. Every chance he gets when he thinks no one is watching, he is running his eyes over you."

"I am sure he does that with all the females. He has only been around the Sarnonn, and we must be more to his liking," said Tehya.

"I think it is more. He seems a little obsessed with

you. That, along with his temper, makes a dangerous combination," said Mapiya.

Adia changed the subject. "So, are you hoping for a male or a female?"

"For Khon'Tor's sake, I hope it is a male. And I hope it looks just like him!"

"I need to see you more often now," directed Adia. "And let me know if anything changes, or if you have any discomfort."

"Is there anything we can do to help you, Tehya?" asked Mapiya.

"I could use some larger, warmer wrappings. Nowadays, I feel cold in Kthama, and I am outgrowing all I have. Now I wish I had let Oh'Dar make me something more like what he wears."

"You know Oh'Dar is happy for you to use his workroom. There are lots of hides, furs, and even the Brothers' fabrics in there. Pakuna wears wrappings, and she is good at patterns. I am sure she would be glad to help you," suggested Adia.

"Thank you. I would appreciate the help. And if anyone could make suggestions as to what I should do to our quarters to prepare for the offspring?" asked Tehya.

Adia became quiet, remembering how Kachina had prepared the Leader's Quarters for Nootau after the High Council forced her to give up her offspring. She had to remind herself that Nootau was safe and now a grown young male, well past pairing age.

Acaraho came over behind her and put his hands

on her shoulders, leaned in, and whispered, "We have another date tonight, remember? So please do not work too long and fall asleep on me like the other night."

"I am sorry. Just too much on my mind," she said.

"Well, it does not do much for a male's confidence when his female dozes off just as he is about to—"

"Sssh!" Adia laughed. "I promise. Tonight I will stay awake, at least until you are done," she whispered back.

"Well, if it is not a *bother*," he teased her back quietly.

Adia was enjoying their banter—happy that they were paired at last and could openly enjoy their relationship.

Tehya gently interrupted the two. "Adia, do you think I could start using his workshop right away? You have me excited about making some new wrappings. Maybe I can even make some for Khon'Tor."

All the females broke out in laughter.

"Khon'Tor, wearing wrappings like the elderly males? Oh my, that is hilarious. Well, who knows, Tehya? He just might. I believe he would do anything for you," said Nadiwani. "I am going to open the workshop and look around," she continued. "I know where everything is in there; come on down when you are ready."

For a while, Tehya remained with the females in the common area, enjoying the camaraderie. Then she went to tell Khon'Tor where she was going. He was not too far away, speaking with some of the males. He had stayed where he could keep an eye on her, though with Akar'Tor sequestered away, he was considerably more relaxed.

Tehya approached her mate. "Excuse me, Adoeete," she said, touching his arm. Towering over her, he immediately looked down.

"I asked you not to call me that." Turning to the others, he added, "I do not know why I try; she does not listen," and they laughed good-humoredly.

Tehya also laughed, and continued, "I am going with Nadiwani to Oh'Dar's workshop to play with the materials."

Khon'Tor nodded, and as she left, she turned and smiled back at him.

The males looked at each other, all thinking how much Khon'Tor had changed. *But could such a drastic turnaround be permanent?*

Khon'Tor took his leave to follow Tehya to the workshop.

When the pair was out of sight, one of the males voiced what they were all thinking. "It is that little mate who has changed him. Should something happen to her, Great Spirit, help us all."

CHAPTER 3

Haan had called everyone into a group just outside the main cave at Kayerm. Tension was thick in the air.

"You are aware that some time ago, Hakani, Akar, and I left Kayerm for a while," he began. "What you did not know is that we went to find the Akassa. Akar was very ill and not improving, and I decided that the Healer at Kthama was the only hope to save his and Hakani's lives. You have seen our offling. She would not be alive without the help of the Akassa—and neither would Akar."

The severity of what Haan had done rolled through the crowd like a shock wave. They knew that their Leader had taken his Akassa mate and adopted son and left, but no one had known where they were going.

Frozen statues stood looking at Haan, their eyes wide with fear. He continued, "The Akassa have paid a great price for helping us. The sickness that ran through Kayerm took a far heavier toll on them. There is no doubt that Hakani, Akar'Tor, and I brought it with us. They lost many of their males with potential longer-term consequences for those who survived."

Still reeling from the realization that their Leader had intentionally broken Sacred Law, no one said anything.

Finally, Yar spoke up. "It is true; I have seen their males. They are not a great threat to us."

Murmurs now rolled through the crowd. Finally, someone shouted out, "All our lives, our fathers' lives, and those before them, we were warned we must never let them know of our existence. We are forbidden to have contact with them, and we are lucky still to be here after you rescued her!" And he pointed at Hakani.

"We have been over and over this, Tarnor. There were signs that affirmed my action in saving her, and you know it.

"And though you may purely think it a selfish act on my part, there is more to it. We are at a breaking point. We know we need to bring in other blood, or our offling will deteriorate. Long ago, we shared a common root with the Akassa, but our people separated. You know this. We were forbidden by the Rah'hora to contact them. But our situation is now desperate. Our only hope lies with them."

"So what of the Fathers-Of-Us-All? They threatened to destroy us if we contacted the Akassa," shouted another.

Haan waited for the conversation to die down. "Either way, we perish. I prefer to die trying rather than to sit here and watch our females bear offling with worse and worse deformities."

"What is your plan then, Adik'Tar?" Tarnor spat out the title like an expletive.

"The Akassa are facing the same problems, but are willing to help us. Their Healer died without passing down the information about Kthama Minor, and their understanding of our past is inaccurate and incomplete, so they also need our help. It is up to us to restore to them the full knowledge of the Wrak-Wavara." He paused. "I am going to open Kthama Minor."

Upheaval broke out.

"Adik'Tar, you do not know what you are doing!"

"This is madness."

"We will all die!"

Haan drew himself up to his full height, and his eyes flashed. "We are all going to die at some point, anyway. *That is a fact.* But this is our only chance of a future for our offling—and theirs. I will give you time to consider your positions. Those who are with me, I will need your help, and we must prepare ourselves before we can open Kthama Minor. Those of you who are against me, if you are afraid, you are free to leave with your families."

Massive dark-haired bodies shifted and turned,

arms flailing, voices raised as they shouted over each other in the din.

Seeing his community split and in an uproar, Haan felt the anguish that Moc'Tor, the Mothoc legend who led them through the Wrak-Wavara, must have felt. But he knew in his heart that this was the right path—the only path—forward.

"Why should *we* leave? You brought this on us by taking Hakani back to Kthama! You should go live at Kthama and take the wrath of the Mothoc with you," accused Tarnor.

Haan stepped in front of Hakani, who was holding Kalli. "Would you have allowed her and my unborn daughter to die a horrible death? Is that who you have become, Tarnor? Asking the Akassa for help did not cause our problems. Instead, it has provided the path for our salvation. *They are willing to help us,*" answered Haan.

The Sarnonn Healer, Artadel, stepped forward to speak. "Saving Hakani and Akar'Tor was beyond my abilities. This is a fact. The only hope for them lay with the Akassa Healer. Yes, the law forbidding contacting the Akassa has been broken. This is also a fact. But whether it was a law for all time, we do not know. Our situation is dire; we must change, or we will perish, and this is a fact too. Quiet yourselves and listen to your hearts. You will find the answer there. Join us or not, but you must each recognize that the path you choose is up to you alone."

Artadel's words flew true to the heart of each member of the community, and the crowd quieted.

Haan stepped forward again. "As Artadel said, search your hearts. Make your choice—live in fear, waiting for the death you believe is coming, or march forward with me and choose a future for your offling. Those of you who are with me, let me know before the new moon. It will take some time to prepare for what we are about to do."

Haan took Hakani with Kalli still in her arms, and left Kayerm, preferring to find solace somewhere else outdoors than to return to their quarters.

Once they were a safe way from the entrance, Hakani could stay quiet no longer.

"Haan. I barely know anything of what you said in there. What is Kthama Minor, and *what law* forbids you to have anything to do with the People?"

"Our law, the law of the Fathers given to us when my people and yours parted ways," he explained. "After I rescued you, I admonished the community never to speak of the Wrak-Wavara to you or around you, just as I told you never to mention or speak of Kthama and your past. Then I learned from Khon'Tor and the others that the Akassa seem to know nothing of our true history together. At Kthama, I did my best to explain it to the members of their High Council."

"You have to tell me what you told the High Council so I can be prepared," she pleaded. "I have never seen your people upset like this. I am frightened for Kalli—*and* Akar and me."

"My people are your people, Hakani. They would never harm you or Kalli, or Akar," chided Haan.

"I am not afraid of your people. I am afraid of what *by the Great Spirit are the Mothoc!*"

Haan considered her point a moment. "Come," he said and extended his hand to her.

He led Hakani down to one of her favorite spots by the Great River, where he scooped up leaves and soft brush and made a cozy spot for her and Kalli on the thick moss that grew along the bank.

"There. Get comfortable. I will tell you what I told the High Council and we can go from there. It is right that you should know."

Haan told Hakani what he had told Khon'Tor and the others—how the Mothoc were the Fathers-Of-Us-All, how they faced problems with uncontrolled mating and overpopulation. He told her about the sickness that wiped out so many of them as punishment for their foolish overbreeding, and the resultant demand of the females to crossbreed with the Others to save their race. Finally, he explained how two branches were formed and how they eventually separated—those who had become the People staying at Kthama, and his people moving to Kayerm.

She listened patiently before asking any questions.

"So, we share the same laws?"

"I believe they are almost identical. They were decided upon before we parted. The difference seems to be in the last one—whereas yours says to have no contact with Outsiders, ours specifically forbids us to have contact with the Akassa, the People."

"I do not see the difference. All know the laws. If direct knowledge of the Sassen was supposed to be kept secret except to a few, you could not exactly be named, could you? They had to use an obscure term like *Outsiders*," Hakani stated.

Haan blinked, realizing that what she said could be true.

"But what about second laws?" she continued.

"We do not have any second laws. What are those?" he asked.

"The second laws establish the leadership hierarchy. They set the Leader as the highest rank and give him the authority to choose his own mate. All others should be paired through the High Council. It used to say that neither the Healer nor the Healer's Helper could be paired or have offling. And the last is that no female can be taken Without Her Consent."

Haan listened intently. *We have no rule about mating; perhaps that is why we are in trouble now. Even though apparently the Akassa structure their matings—pairings—their lifespans are shorter, so it*

makes sense that while there are more of them, they
could end up in the same place we are at about the same
time. Not enough diversity to ensure healthy offling in
the future.

"It must have been a surprise to the High Council, but why have I never heard any of this, Haan? It explains why you would never talk to me about the People and told me not to discuss them either. I thought you just did not want me stewing about it, as you said. And so I never brought them up."

"Only a few of the Akassa know the story. But knowledge of Kthama Minor was only passed down from Healer to Healer. And I believe that the previous Healer died before she could pass the history on to Adia, so it was lost to Khon'Tor's community."

"I see. But Haan, I still do not understand the Sassen's fear of the Mothoc and being forbidden to have contact with the People—the Akassa." she pointed out.

"The People and the Sassen made different choices. The Mothoc wanted to protect the Sassen from contamination by the Akassa's beliefs, lest our people follow their ways and become even more like them. They wanted to preserve what was left of their blood. And they wanted to protect the Akassa from conflict with the Sassen, knowing that in a clash between us, the Akassa would not survive. They made a Rah'hora with both sides."

"So, they threatened the Sassen with annihilation

if they broke the agreement, and they wiped out any direct knowledge that the Akassa had of you?"

"Yes. And it has been very effective. We have kept ourselves hidden from the Akassa as further protection for both tribes."

"We did not know you still existed. It had been generations since the People saw any Sarnonn," she concurred. "But a Rah'hora is agreed upon by both sides. It sounds like this was a threat, not an agreement."

"A Rah'hora is a contract. It does not require agreement when the balance of power is so one-sided—only compliance."

Hakani shifted her position to get more comfortable. They had been sitting a while.

"And that is what everyone is afraid of—that because we made contact with my people, the Mothoc will annihilate us all?"

"Yes."

Silence.

"There is only one problem with that theory, Haan. If the Mothoc were going to destroy the Sassen for making contact with the Akassa, should they not have done so when you rescued me nearly twenty years ago? Did you not violate the Rah'hora then?"

Haan sighed. *I have struggled off and on with this since the day I found Hakani. Even though there were many reassurances from the Great Spirit that I had chosen correctly, the concerns in the community never fully abated—no doubt kept alive by Tarnor.*

"I do not know the answer to that," Haan said. "Our laws require us to help the sick and injured, and there were particular signs that I was doing the right thing. Perhaps because I did not intentionally contact your kind, the Fathers overlooked my transgression."

Haan fell silent, lost in a struggle with the same question that had haunted him for years.

Days passed. Haan and his Healer, Artadel, planned for the preparation ritual. It was a cool evening, and both sat around a comforting night fire with the bright stars twinkling overhead.

"We do not know what we will find when we open Kthama Minor," explained Artadel. "We are assuming it was not destroyed before it was sealed and cloaked, and that the inside was left intact. If so, the Wall of Records will have survived."

"I hope it answers more questions than it raises. Once the Akassa fully understand what was done and who we are, it may take them some time to adjust. They were already struggling with what I told them during their High Council meeting," answered Haan.

"Perhaps its secrecy has served its purpose—if the Wall of Records is intact, then I believe they knew we would arrive back in the same situation eventually. Overbred and looking for answers.

Whoever sealed Kthama Minor planned it ahead of time, and would have had ample opportunity to destroy the Wall of Records if they had wished."

"I agree, Artadel; we do not know if the law forbidding contact was meant for all time. The Mothoc had to realize it would again come to this."

"Perhaps so, but they would never sanction what happened during the Age of Darkness, not ever again," said the Healer.

Silence.

"Artadel, you are my trusted counselor."

The Healer nodded and waited.

Haan paced while he spoke, his brow tightly furrowed. "Hakani said something to me a little while ago, right after I announced that we were going to open Kthama Minor for the Akassa." Haan stopped and turned to face Artadel.

"And she asked the same question that haunted me when I first found her;

did I not break the Rah'hora when I rescued her?"

"I was at your side through all of it. I was there with you, looking after her. I was there when you told the community what you had done. The sixth law commands that we care for the sick and helpless. And there were signs," Artadel replied, referring to the black crow, which the Sarnonn believed was sent by the Great Spirit as a reminder of their duty to uphold Sacred Law.

Haan nodded his head, "Yes. Ravu'Bahl was there

when I first dragged Hakani from the river, and every day after that for forty days."

"The Great Spirit sends Ravu'Bahl as a reminder of our duty to uphold Sacred Law. Your finding her was possibly indeed divinely ordained, or, because you did not seek her out, finding her did not break the Rah'hora. Other possibilities are that the Mothoc no longer care or they have forgiven us, or that the prohibition was just a tactic for a period until some other goal was achieved. Or perhaps the story about contact is only partly true, or was never true—" Artadel rattled off all the permutations he could think of.

"—or the Mothoc no longer walk Etera," finished Haan.

"The only thing we know is that if the contract was broken years ago—well—we are still here."

Haan sat back down and poked at the fire with a stick, the embers flaring up again in bright orange.

"This is why you are my closest adviser, Artadel," said Haan.

"You are under a great deal of strain, and you are too hard on yourself. Trust your reasoning, listen to your heart, and harness your will to take the path they laid out." Artadel changed the subject. "Have you heard anything of Akar'Tor?"

"No. Hakani and I may have to pay a visit, to ease her mind," answered Haan.

"I thought the Akassa females still had the seventh sense."

"They do, but only to a certain extent, and it seems to become clouded when strong emotions are involved," he explained. "I have seen it many times with Hakani. You have met only her and Akar, but you can see that the Akassa are smaller, weaker, not as protected from the elements. As they brought in more and more of the Others' blood, the best traits of the Fathers were diluted. The males seem to have lost the seventh sense, and by our measures, only a few of the females have any to speak of. From what I picked up, it serves only to give them premonitions and warnings. We are all that is left of the true power of the Mothoc and their responsibility to Etera. But even that is now at risk."

The males sat silent for a moment.

"How did their Adik'Tar, Khon'Tor, accept Akar'-Tor?" asked Artadel.

"There is bad history between Khon'Tor and Hakani; I did not realize how much until I visited Kthama. She has not been herself since we returned. And she has now turned Akar's mind against Khon'-Tor. I do not see Akar being accepted at Kthama, but to a large extent, that is his own fault. No doubt he will be back soon, hopefully less arrogant and a little humbler, but I have my doubts."

"When you and Hakani return, we and those who have decided to join us will begin preparations to open Kthama Minor," said the Healer. "I hope there will be enough of us because I imagine it is not going to be easy. Neither you nor I fully know what to expect when we initiate the Ror'Eckrah."

Both males fell silent and sat waiting for the rest of the logs to burn down to embers before smothering them and turning in.

CHAPTER 4

Nimida and Mapiya were in Mapiya's quarters, restuffing their sleeping mats for the coming winter. Mapiya's two sons had moved out long ago, so when she took Nimida under her wing, she had let the young female move in with her, and they got along so well that the arrangement had lasted.

Nimida was grateful for the warm relationship that had grown between her and the older female. After her mother's death, Nimida had missed having someone to lean on who cared about her. Her mother's sister was not a warm person, and Nimida's life had become difficult. When the Healer and Nadiwani had offered to let her stay at the High Rocks, it was an easy decision—there was nothing left for her back at the Great Pines.

"So, tell me; of everything you have learned, what is your favorite skill?" asked Mapiya as they continued to stuff fresh grasses and sweet-smelling herbs into one of the mats.

"I enjoy weaving; it relaxes my mind. But my favorite is honing the stones to sharp points for spears and blades. Is that unusual?"

"I do not think so. As you know, many of our expert tool makers are females. I can see where there would be satisfaction in that. Everyone has different aptitudes and preferences. It is simply about finding what gives you joy!"

"I love the sound the hammer stone makes against the flint and seeing the sharp flakes fall away. So far, I have not cut myself too badly, either," she laughed.

Finished with the one mat, they turned to the other.

"We will enjoy sinking into these when they are done! I do not know why we do not re-stuff them more often," noted Mapiya.

"It is a lot easier with two working together," and Nimida smiled at Mapiya.

"Always remember that you are welcome to stay with me as long as you like. You know that I never had a daughter and that I enjoy your company. Of course, when you think of pairing, I will certainly understand that you need to move out."

"I am happy as we are, Mapiya. There is no one I am interested in. I am in no rush to take on the problems of a male ordering me around," she shared.

"Is that what it is like at the Great Pines? Are the males there very bossy?"

"Many of them are. They all seemed to have strong personalities. And they are so much larger than almost everyone here. They also have far more body covering. My father was stern with my mother, but she was the kindest soul. He did not need to be so abrupt. It was just his personality, but I felt sorry for her. I would not take it as she did; I am afraid I would fight with any male who tried to order me around. For that reason, after she was gone, tensions rose between him and me."

Mapiya looked at the young female. Nimida had always seemed mild-mannered to her.

"Are you still glad that it did not work out with you and Nootau? At the Ashwea Awhidi?"

"Yes, I am. After my mother died, I waited anxiously for an Ashwea Awhidi to be announced. Being paired was the only way for me to leave the Great Pines, even knowing I could be trading one problem for another if the High Council had not chosen well for me. Nootau is a nice male and a great friend, but now I am glad I have the opportunity to figure out what I really want before making such a big decision," she explained.

She paused before continuing.

"After my mother died, until his passing, my father turned his frustration onto me. They never had any other offspring, so there was no one else on whom to deflect his irritation. I never did feel I fitted in. My mother's sister, Kinya, who came with me to the Ashwea Awhidi, took me in, but we never bonded."

Mapiya did not want to pry. It was the first time Nimida had opened up to her so deeply about her personal life at the Great Pines, and she did not want to push it.

"Anyway, Nootau and I are great friends. He helped me adjust. I am not sure if he was disappointed, but it worked out for the best. He has always felt more like a brother to me than anything else," she continued.

I am sure Adia will be disappointed to hear that, Mapiya said to herself. *I think she hoped that maybe in time, it would still work out for them. Adia seems to take a special interest in Nimida. She and Nadiwani spend a lot of time with her, and they all seem to get along well. But maybe that is why Nimida thinks of Nootau as a brother. Between us, we pretty much adopted her from the first moment she came here.*

"I do not know if I want to be paired and have offspring. I know that probably sounds wrong," added Nimida.

"You are still very young. You have lots of time to decide that. And if it turns out you do not want to be joined, there is nothing wrong with that, either. We have some bachelors who choose not to be paired. Sometimes they change their minds, and sometimes they do not. Not everyone has a strong mating drive or a need to raise offspring. Akule is a good example.

He never wanted to pair, but I think the relationship between Adia and Acaraho changed his mind. He and his new mate seem settled now. She came to us at the last Ashwea Awhidi, just as you did."

"Yes, Kayah is very nice. She keeps to herself quite a bit, but then I guess I do too. I think I would like to be friends with Tehya. Do you think the Leader's choice makes friends like that? She seems so very kind to everyone, but of those of us her age, the only one she seems particularly close to is Oh'Dar. And she is so beautiful. I love that she has all those different wrappings! Most of us seem to wear the same designs."

"There is no reason you cannot be friends with Tehya. I am sure she would love to have more female company. There is only one way to find out if you hit it off, and that is to spend time with her. I understand she is going to be using Oh'Dar's workshop to make some new wrappings because she has outgrown those she has."

"Alright. I will do it. You have given me confidence. I will make friends with Tehya!"

"Do you want to see if they are in Oh'Dar's workshop now?"

"Yes!"

So the two females quickly finished off the last sleeping mat and headed for the workshop.

Nadiwani opened the door and waited for Tehya to show up. She flipped through the skins wondering which ones the Leader's mate would pick out for herself.

She and Adia showed up shortly, Kweeuu trotting alongside them. Adia felt her heart sink as she entered the workshop. It made her miss Oh'Dar so much she could hardly stand it.

"Oh, Adia. I am so sorry; I have been thoughtless. I did not even think of how this might affect you. I should not have asked," Tehya cried out.

Adia squeezed back tears. "No. Oh'Dar would be very happy to have you make use of his workshop. It is exactly what he would want. He will come back someday, and you can show him what you made— and your new offspring."

Nadiwani called them over to the stack of hides. "Look at these."

Tehya ran her hands over the soft fur, so luxurious.

"Those would keep you warm."

"They are beautiful. I noticed them before. I do not think I could wear them though—what would Kweeuu think?" she asked, and they laughed. But then from the look on her face, they realized she was serious.

"That is so sweet. But I do not believe Kweeuu would think anything at all! He doesn't seem to mind the fur sleeping cover, does he?" pointed out Adia. She almost slipped up and suggested that Urilla

Wuti could try to find out, remembering the stirring between Kweeuu and Oh'Dar that the Healer had created.

"You are right; he does seem to like it. He wallows all over it every time he gets the chance," joked Tehya.

"Remember that the winter winds are coming," said Nadiwani. "You may not need such warm wrappings inside Kthama, but perhaps if you go outside?"

"That is a good point. I will consider it."

Before long, Pakuna showed up with Nimida and Mapiya, and the females started going through the materials together and deciding on patterns.

Nimida held up a soft caramel-colored deer hide. "Look, Tehya! This would be beautiful on you. It is almost the same color as your hair. And it would go perfectly with that necklace with the amber stones." she exclaimed, referring to the necklace Khon'Tor had given her.

Adia put her arm around Nimida, smiling at her kindness.

"What do you think, Pakuna? Could you help Tehya make something with this that would keep her warmer?"

"I am sure I could. Do you want it for now while you are with offspring—or for later after you get your figure back?" she asked.

"That is a good point—for later, I think, yes. But I need something now to keep me warmer *and* give me more room until our offspring arrives," Tehya agreed.

"What about you, Nimida? When will you be paired?" asked Pakuna.

Nadiwani saw Adia stiffen and look down quickly.

"Mapiya and I were just talking about that. I am not sure I ever want to pair," she admitted.

"But you and Nootau are so close. And the High Council picked you for each other!"

"Yes, I do love Nootau—"

Adia's heart stopped.

"—but not like that. He is more like a brother to me."

Adia's heart started beating again—

"I felt like that from the start. We have a lot of fun together, but I do not look at him as a potential mate," Nimida confessed. "I guess because you and Adia took me under your wing—and Mapiya—that you all feel like family to me. I am happy with how things are now."

The females spent the next few hours chatting and laughing together. When it was time to go, Tehya spoke up. "Would anyone else like to meet here again? I have enjoyed your company—I mean, if you would want to," she asked tentatively.

Everyone agreed, and they made plans to start meeting at least once a week to have some female time together.

"Maybe we can invite Urilla Wuti next time?" suggested Adia, and everyone agreed. Tehya was especially happy since she and the older Healer were both from the community of the Far High Hills.

Adia walked away, thinking over what Nimida had said about Nootau. *Thank the Mother,* she thought. *But the relationship between them is only part of it. It doesn't mean I can let things stay as they are forever. She has a right to know that I am her mother. And the truth about her relationship to Nootau.*

Down the hallway, Akar'Tor was sulking in his room.

The young male had not made any friends at Kthama. His life consisted mostly of his lessons, eating alone in his room, and planning how to thwart the guards. The rest of the time he spent in the Great Chamber, listening and learning, picking up any possible tidbits about Tehya and her daily schedule. When he could observe Khon'Tor unnoticed, Akar'Tor studied him in depth. Later in the privacy of his quarters, he practiced copying the Leader's walk, his stance, his body language, his facial expressions. Before too long, Akar'Tor thought he could do a pretty good job of mimicking his father. Not enough to pass in broad daylight, but—maybe enough to get him where he wanted to be—alone with Tehya with no one to stop him from making her his.

He had put a plan together and was waiting for the opportunity to present itself.

◐

After the announcement of Tehya's seeding, Khon'Tor kept his distance from Akar'Tor. The training continued, and Khon'Tor made sure that none of it was to the young male's liking.

◐

"Acaraho, give me your assessment of Akar," the Leader said one day as they were meeting together.

"He has apparently resigned himself to living in isolation. He does take meals in the common area, sitting alone, but he seems to be taking in everything said and going on around him From my observations and what the guards have reported to me, he has stayed away from Tehya completely since the confrontation after you announced that she is with offspring, He does not even look in her direction. You, however—"

"I have noticed. No doubt plotting his revenge. What else?"

"Do you still not think you have enough cause to oust him from Kthama?" asked Acaraho.

"I admit my self-control around him is stretched

thin. I have stayed away since that day because of it. I am not sure what I am waiting for," Khon'Tor said.

"I mean no offense, Khon'Tor. But you usually do not have any difficulty making a decision," Acaraho pointed out. "Considering how he has behaved, no one is going to fault you for sending him back to Kayerm."

"I did not start out hating him; he achieved that on his own. And the longer he stays, the higher the chances are that I will hurt him badly before it is over. You are right. I must get him out of here before I do something that destroys our relationship with Haan. He will never be my son, but in all the ways that matter, he *is* Haan's."

Khon'Tor paused and ran his hand through his silver crown.

"Make the signal break. When the Sarnonn messenger shows up, tell them to ask Haan to come and take Akar home. Since his father seems to be the only one he will listen to, I would not trust sending him home with the messenger."

"Very well," said Acaraho. "I will go to the valley tomorrow."

Khon'Tor retired to his quarters, a big grin crossing his face when he spotted his mate. Tehya was sitting cross-legged on their sleeping mat, playing with some little stones that she had arranged in front of her.

"Adoeete! Come see!" she squealed.

He leaned down to peer at the pile of rich colors in front of her.

"Adia showed me where Oh'Dar keeps his beads. Pakuna is going to help me make me a new wrapping out of the most beautiful deer hide. And once Oh'Dar returns and says it is alright to use them, if I am not able to sew them in place, I will ask him to do so."

Khon'Tor sat down behind her and straddled her with his legs as he often did at the eating table. He looked over her shoulder as she pushed the shiny rocks around into different patterns, his body enfolding hers protectively. She held up one after another, showing him her favorites.

He kissed her on the neck, then buried his nose in her hair, inhaling her sweet scent and enjoying the feel of her soft curls against his face. Just as she had the stones arranged, he snatched the center one away.

"Hey," she laughed, looking back at him over her shoulder. "You took the best one."

"Of course I did. I know a jewel when I see one— I picked you, did I not?"

"What do I have to do to get it back?"

"Oh, I am sure I can think of *something*—" and he leaned in and whispered in her ear, "I so miss claiming you—that sweet moment of surrender, when I take my position above you, and you part your legs for me. And when I press myself against you, I can feel how ready you are, wanting me, baring yourself, just waiting for me to thrust my—"

"By the Mother, Adoeete, *stop!*" Tehya turned and put her fingers on his lips, full color coming to her cheeks.

"Am I embarrassing you?" Khon'Tor chuckled, knowing full well he was.

"Yes! Sssh!" she laughed.

"Do you not like it when I talk about it? Should I not tell you what I want to do to you once our offspring is born? I promise you will enjoy it, and I will take my time to make sure you do," he whispered. He could hear her breathing deepening, despite her protestations.

"If you trust me, there are ways I can please you that you have no idea of yet, little mate."

He took her hand and held it while he slowly laced his tongue around and through her fingers.

Her eyes grew wide, and she held her breath.

He stopped and smiled, "Do not worry, we have lots of time for this. The most important thing is that you and our offspring are alright. Everything else can wait."

And he kissed her palm and gave her back the beautiful red carnelian bead he had snatched from her arrangement.

"What did you do today?" he asked.

She placed it back in the center of her pattern, "I

spent the afternoon with some of the females in Oh'Dar's workshop. Mapiya, Adia, Nadiwani, Pakuna, and Nimida. We had a wonderful time. Every season I feel less like the isolated Leader's mate and more like part of the community of females here. Adia has been so kind to me, Khon'Tor. And Nadiwani too. They have made me feel like family right from the first day. I am grateful for their kindness and I would like to meet with them regularly. Pakuna is going to help me make some larger warm wrappings. Ever since I was sick, I do get cold in here more often," she said.

"Well then, come here and let me warm you as I did then. You were so fragile. I was never more afraid in my whole life," he mused out loud, then added, "I am pleased you are making friends."

Tehya scooped up her treasures and put them in the pouch Pakuna had made for them, tucked them under her side of the mat, and curled up next to Khon'Tor. She never felt as safe as she did when she was with him. No matter what else might be going on, this was her place of refuge and sanctuary. She rested her head on his shoulder and listened to his deep breathing. *I am so happy. Who knew I could be so happy.*

Just before she drifted off to sleep, Tehya felt Kweeuu curl up against her back.

CHAPTER 5

Acaraho tromped through the long grasses in the valley, the scent of the damp soil from the overnight rain rising as the ground squished under his feet. It was a beautiful late-summer morning. Bird song lilted from the tree-tops. White puffy clouds shielded the heat of the sun, which was already climbing. He found the right place and made the mark signaling that they wanted to make contact with Haan's people. He looked around before turning back, listening. He did not feel he was being watched as he had other times. *Perhaps Adia was right; perhaps it was Akar'Tor watching us those times before. But he will not be at Kthama for much longer.*

Once back, Acaraho went to find Khon'Tor.

The Leader was standing in a circle, speaking with some of the guards. As Acaraho approached, they moved up to include him.

"It is done," the High Protector told Khon'Tor. Now we wait."

To the males, he said, "Alert the watchers that we are expecting a return of a Sarnonn and alert the Adik'Tar when someone arrives. We are hoping Haan will come. It is time for Akar'Tor to return to Kayerm. "

Khon'Tor stepped away, and Acaraho followed after dismissing the guards. They headed for the eating area.

"It would be simpler if Haan comes himself, rather than having to send a messenger back for him," observed Khon'Tor.

"Since Haan will be here at some point, I am concerned about the knowledge lost with Lifrin's death," said Acaraho. "The secrets passed down through the generations by the High Rocks Healers. The secrets that died with Lifrin before Adia got here."

"The loss of Lifrin's knowledge may not be crucial. Haan has revealed more about our history than we have certainly ever heard before, and has made us realize how much of what we understood was wrong," Khon'Tor said. "The Age of Shadows for one; first, the High Council thought it was the Waschini, then we thought it was the threat of extinction due to the dwindling pool of our blood-line. Now it may turn out to be something utterly different—a broken Rah'hora between our people and others we were not even sure still existed."

"Since the Sarnonn live longer than we do, yes—there is a greater chance that his information is correct. I am sure there is always some distortion when history is told and re-told over multiple generations," said Acaraho. "As to the truth of what Wrak-Ayya is—well, we may only know when it does descend."

The eating area was emptying as they seated themselves at Khon'Tor's official table. It was situated away from the rest and now reserved mainly for serious discussion. Within a few moments, one of the females brought them some of the last remaining food.

"Thank you, Kachina," said Khon'Tor, looking up to see Tehya approaching.

As Tehya took her spot next to him, he put his arm around her and slipped it under her hip, pulling her up against him. He slid a portion of the food in front of her.

"I was just speaking with Acaraho's charges, and letting them know that Akar will be leaving soon."

"Akar'Tor is leaving? When?" she asked.

"Acaraho sent a message for Haan's people to make contact—so as soon as Haan can come and collect him." He looked at her soft lips as he spoke, wanting to bite them gently. *This is excruciating, waiting until I can take her again.*

Tehya could tell what he was thinking and glared at him. "*Stop it*," she scolded him playfully under her breath.

Acaraho excused himself. "I will leave you to
your meal."

After the High Protector was gone, Khon'Tor said,
"You are not eating."

"I was going to, but someone has caused me to
become distracted."

"Are you easily distracted?" he continued their
banter.

"Not usually. But I think I could eat now if my
tormentor would allow it," and she looked at him
with sparkling eyes.

"Torment, is it? Is that what I am doing to you?
The look on your face tells a different story. Make no
mistake. As soon as you give me your consent after
our offspring is born—" As his voice trailed off, he
lifted her chin to him and kissed her, lingering
slightly longer than was appropriate in public, but
the hall was empty.

Except, Khon'Tor was wrong. The hall was not
entirely empty. And the one watching was not happy
about their display. Not at all.

Unknown to either Acaraho, Khon'Tor, or Tehya,
Akar'Tor was watching them from the food preparation area. In the stir about contacting Haan, neither
Khon'Tor nor Acaraho had checked his work
schedule for that day.

Akar'Tor did not like what the Leader was doing

to Tehya one bit. If he could have heard their conversation, he would have moved up the execution of his plan.

Khon'Tor glanced up and caught the young male staring at them. His anger flared, and he rose to his feet.

"*No more.* Tehya, stay here."

He strode to the food preparation area and grabbed Akar'Tor by the arm, jerking him into the Great Chamber and pushing him onto the rock floor. Within seconds, Acaraho and Akar'Tor's two assigned guards were there.

"Escort him to his quarters. He is not to leave until I say so. Arrange for food to be brought to him, but that is all. Understood?"

Each guard took one side of Akar'Tor and dragged him to his feet. Khon'Tor watched, unmoving, as they took him away.

The Leader turned to Acaraho. "I do not care if Haan does not come for a year. Make sure that *PetaQ* does not leave his quarters."

Yar found the tree break as he was making the rounds of his watch. He returned immediately to Kayerm.

"Adik'Tar, forgive the interruption. The Akassa would like contact."

"When did they signal?" asked Haan.

"Based on the age of the strip, a few days ago," answered Yar.

Haan turned to his mate, "Do you wish to go with me?"

"Yes. I can leave Kalli with Haaka. When will we leave?" asked Hakani.

"We will travel late tonight so we can be there at first light."

Hakani nodded and asked Yar to fetch Haaka so they could make arrangements. "I will be ready."

Well after nightfall, Haan and Hakani set out. Yar and two others went with them in line with the protocol accorded their Adik'Tar and his mate. As they walked, Hakani's thoughts returned to the life she had left behind at Kthama.

So hard to go back. So many wounds re-opened. I would rather not see Khon'Tor or his new mate. I wish I had never returned; I wish I had not convinced Haan to take us there. Even though I would probably have died, at least I had found some relative peace at Kayerm. I cannot seem to get it back now that these old wounds are open again. What is wrong with me? One moment I want to return peacefully to whatever life I can have with Haan, and at the next, I have these wild fantasies of destroying Khon'Tor and taking over Kthama.

By first light, they had reached their destination.

The watchers notified Awan that several figures were approaching. One appeared to be Haan and the other Hakani. Two good-sized Sarnonn traveling with them had stopped a way back and seemed to be waiting there. Word was sent to Khon'Tor and Acaraho, both of whom went to the Great Entrance to meet the visitors. They were unpleasantly surprised to see that Hakani was there too.

Seething inside that she had the gall to return, Khon'Tor refused to look at her. *I thought I made it clear that Hakani has no place here. I trust he has a very good reason for including her.*"

"Greetings, Adik'Tar 'Tor," said Haan.

"Welcome back, Adik'Tar Haan. Thank you for coming. Would you like to rest before we speak?"

"I will leave that decision to my mate," replied Haan, but Hakani said nothing.

"I asked you to come to take Akar back home with you. It is not going to work for him to stay at Kthama," Khon'Tor replied, adding no apologies.

"This is not a surprise. He tried to claim by will that which can only be earned. Where is he now?"

"He has been confined to his quarters pending your arrival," answered Acaraho.

Haan nodded.

"Do you wish to lodge overnight before returning?" Khon'Tor did not want to make the offer but reminded himself that the budding relationship between himself and the Sarnonn Leader was of crucial importance.

Haan turned to Hakani.

"No. I am anxious to see Akar and get him home." She tried to avoid looking at Khon'Tor in an attempt to keep her rising anger at bay.

Acaraho signed to Awan, who went to fetch Akar'Tor.

"When we parted, there was talk about preparation," said Khon'Tor as they waited, carefully not mentioning Kthama Minor.

"I am in the process of doing that; it may be some time. Your Healers should also prepare."

"Prepare how?" asked Khon'Tor. *This didn't come up before.*

"The loss of your previous Healer is crippling because she would have passed that knowledge down. They need to prepare," Haan repeated.

He has said that twice with no information about what it means, thought Khon'Tor.

"Shall I bring Adia here, Haan?" asked Acaraho.

"I have no knowledge of the preparation ritual. I only know that one was provided."

Acaraho shot a concerned look at Khon'Tor. "So, whoever sealed it anticipated that at some point, it would be reopened." *Clues, but no answers—only more questions, and now this. Why forbid contact and then leave instructions about what to do if it happened? Or perhaps opening Kthama Minor and making contact with the Sarnonn are two separate issues.*

"Haan, I appreciate your help. I will pass your warning on to Adia, Nadiwani, and Urilla Wuti,"

Khon'Tor replied as the guards returned with Akar'Tor.

The young upstart saw his parents and hurried his steps. He embraced his mother and then Haan.

"We have come to take you home, Akar," Haan explained.

"I am not ready. I need more time. He did not even give me a chance," whined Akar'Tor, looking back at Khon'Tor.

"I do not believe that is true, Akar. But either way, your stay here is over. You will return with us and make peace with your path among our people."

Hakani spoke up, "Akar, did you meet a female here you could take as a mate?"

Akar'Tor narrowed his eyes, wanting to say yes but not daring to. "I have been kept busy with menial chores. There was no opportunity."

Hakani sighed. "Perhaps another time."

Khon'Tor locked eyes with her. "There will be no other time, Hakani. Akar's business here is over. Forever. If he wishes to find a mate, he must do so in one of the other communities up the Mother Stream. He is not welcome back at Kthama," he stated unequivocally. *What would possess her to come back here? She must know she is unwelcome. It is obvious that she has corrupted Akar. With everything that happened between Hakani and me, he never stood a chance of fitting in here. She knows he cannot simply pick a mate! And how does she think I would let any of our females be paired with that arrogant—*

"We are leaving now, Akar. You will come with us," ordered Haan.

"No. I do not want to. My place is here. I should be the next Leader of the High Rocks. It is my right."

Khon'Tor's blood boiled higher, and the edge of his lip curled.

"Leadership is no one's right, Akar. If you do not come with us now, you can never return to Kayerm," Haan said calmly.

Hakani shot Haan a burning look and touched his arm.

The Sarnonn looked down at her. "This is males' business. You do not understand. Choose, Akar," he continued, returning his gaze to the Akassa he had raised as his own.

Akar'Tor scowled and slowly stepped forward to indicate that he would return with them.

Haan turned back to Khon'Tor and Acaraho. "I apologize for whatever trouble he has caused you."

Khon'Tor nodded, holding back the scalding words he wanted to unleash on Akar'Tor. He steeled himself not to look at Hakani again.

"How is your mate, Tehya?" she could not resist asking.

Va! I had hoped Tehya would not come up, Khon'Tor swore to himself.

"He has *seeded* her," Akar'Tor said with a snarl, his eyes fixed on Khon'Tor.

Hakani huffed before she could stop herself.

"Congratulations, Khon'Tor. Perhaps now you

will have a son suitable to lead when you are ready to step down. Come, we are leaving now," and Haan turned, Hakani and their son following him.

Just before Akar'Tor cleared the exit, he looked back and shot a furious glance at Khon'Tor. *There go all my plans,* he thought. *Now I will have to think of another way to make Tehya mine.*

"Well, that went positively," said Acaraho sarcastically.

"I was hoping Tehya's condition would not come up. It is clear that Hakani still harbors resentment," said Khon'Tor.

"If we did not need their help, we would be best to cut off all contact. But as it is—"

"The needs of the community outweigh the needs of any one of us, and we have to keep moving forward," sighed Khon'Tor, referring to First Law.

"I will tell Adia what Haan said. Perhaps Urilla Wuti will have an idea about how to prepare?" replied Acaraho.

"It is fortunate that Urilla Wuti is still here, and I appreciate her community's sacrifice. Tehya is also glad to have her here because they both come from the Far High Hills."

"Will she stay until Tehya delivers? Because of their history together."

"I will ask her to stay the duration, if Harak'Sar

can spare her longer and if Urilla Wuti is willing," said Khon'Tor.

Haan, Hakani, and Akar'Tor met up with the two Sarnonn who had been waiting down the winding path from Kthama's entrance.

"I am not ready to go back," Akar'Tor repeated as he stomped alongside his father. Haan stopped and turned to the stroppy young male.

"It does not matter whether you are ready or not, Akar. Everything will not happen according to your will. You are headstrong like your mother, this I accept. But your continual challenge of authority must stop. If you do not find a way to check it within yourself, you will run up against others all your life. I had hoped your stay at Kthama would have taught you this."

"If you are talking about Khon'Tor, he never gave me a chance. All I did was female work. I clearly threatened him, and he found an excuse to get rid of me."

Haan shook his head. *What will become of him? We had no choice but to go to Kthama, but Hakani's return stirred up her bitterness, and she has now poisoned Akar's mind as well. I never saw this in him before. He was always broody, kept to himself, but he was not angry all the time. If we did not need the help of the Akassa, and they did not need ours, I would end our contact with*

Kthama now and hope Hakani and Akar both settle down. But as our futures are to be interwoven, it is even more critical that they let go of this obsession with Khon'Tor.

"I can assure you that Khon'Tor is not threatened by you, Akar. He may find you irritating and disrespectful, but an Alpha such as Khon'Tor takes no mind of one such as you. I know my words are hurtful, but you do not hear me unless I am stern with you. If you wish to be respected, then you must start by growing up and letting go of these ridiculous imaginings.

"You are of an age to pair and move on with your life. Put your energy into planning how we can contact the other Akassa communities. Once you are paired, I suspect much of your tension will fade," he continued.

Hakani finally spoke. "Haan, as one of the People, he would be paired by the High Council."

"But he is not one of the People, Hakani. He is Akassa, but he is not one of the People. We must find our own way through this. Now, let us continue on. No doubt Kalli will need her mother back soon," and Haan started moving onward toward Kayerm.

As they returned, just past twilight, Tarnor met them at the entrance.

"We need to talk."

"What is it Tarnor?" Haan looked down at the brother of his first mate. *We seem to be even worse adversaries since Kesta died. I wonder if he blames me for her passing.*

Tarnor glanced over at Hakani and Akar'Tor.

At his look, Haan dismissed them. "I will find you later. I suggest you both rest."

Expecting an argument, Haan then led Tarnor away from the entrance.

"You are outnumbered, Haan. Those who are joining you are far fewer than those who are joining me. *You should be the ones to leave Kayerm*, not us. In this case, you are the rebels. And perhaps if you leave, the Mothoc will spare us."

Haan sighed, too tired to deal with this now. "I have much to do. I do not have time for your argument today. Another time," and Haan started to walk away.

Tarnor grabbed him by the arm and forced him back around. "You do not scare me, *Adik'Tar!*"

Haan looked down at Tarnor's hand and then narrowed his eyes. He grabbed the male's wrist and twisted it, forcing him to let go. "Has everyone here gone mad? What is wrong with you? Ever since Kesta returned to the Great Spirit, you have been even angrier with me than usual. Do you blame me for your sister's passing?"

"No—I blame you for making that abomination your First Choice. She is not fit to be the Leader's mate.

It was bad enough that you rescued her and brought her here, but then you mounted her? You want our future offling to look like that monstrous *creation of yours?*" he raged. "The Akassa should be destroyed."

Haan felled Tarnor with one blow to the gut, and the male crumpled to the ground in agony. Without mercy, Haan pulled him back up and punched him in the face, releasing him to drop to the ground once more. Then the Leader circled him, shouting as Tarnor lay trying to recover.

"Today is not the day for this. If you were not my first mate's brother, I would throw you out of Kayerm right now. What has happened has happened. And I thought I settled this long ago when I first rescued Hakani. I see you now for what you are—a small-minded bigot! The Akassa are of us. They share our heritage. Those we call the Fathers are also *their* Fathers. If you were not blinded by ignorance, you would see that *they* are the future. Now that I have spent time with them, I see first-hand that they are more inventive than us and more resilient. They adapt more easily. They do not have our physical strength or longevity, but in every other way, we are no match for them."

He circled Tarnor as he spoke, "We *need* them, Tarnor. And like it or not, *you and I need each other.* I hate that my people are being divided, just as were the Fathers during the Wrak-Wavara. But if you do not change, your fate is decided. If you do not bring in other seed, your offling will soon be deformed and deadborn."

"This is who we are. And this is who we will stay," snarled Tarnor from where he lay on the floor curled up with one hand to his chin.

"Then you doom all the Sassen to a future of wailing mothers," said Haan. He pictured sobbing mothers gathered around the sinister glow of tiny death pyres, flames licking the night sky.

"If you and your handful love the Akassa so much, you go and live with *them* and leave Kayerm to us."

Haan stiffened and straightened up for a moment, not having thought of that possibility. *Is Tarnor right; are the numbers joining me truly that small? If so, it does make more sense that I and my following leave instead of Tarnor's.*

"I will leave you to your misery, Tarnor. But threaten my family again, or any of the Akassa, and you will be reunited in the Great Spirit with your sister sooner rather than later."

He turned to see Hakani in the entrance, having seen—and heard—everything.

Haan put his arm around her and walked her back inside. He could feel her shaking.

"Is that how they feel about me—about Kalli? Are we not safe here now? Neither of us is any match for them, not even *Akar'Tor*." Her eyes widened with fear.

"No one will harm you," he assured her.

"You cannot be everywhere. If they want to, they will find a way," she answered, remembering her own devious past.

"This is why the Mothoc made the Rah'hora—to protect the Akassa, not the Sassen. The time of unrest and struggle between the Mothoc during the Wrak-Wavara became bloody. But at least the Mothoc were evenly matched. I thought we had evolved past this; in a battle between the Sassen and the Akassa, we know the Akassa will not survive. "

He bowed his head to think. "Perhaps it is we who need to leave. Perhaps there is nothing we can do for Tarnor and his rebels but leave them to their fate. If we leave, there will be no reason for them to come up against your people. We could return to the days of secrecy and separate existence between the Sassen and Akassa."

Haan's shoulders were heavy with the burden he carried. *Despite the sixth law, perhaps my bringing her here did break the Rah'hora, and it has taken this long for the effects to surface. The Mothoc lived for thousands of years, and the time since I rescued her would be the mere blink of an eye to them.*

He looked up. "Where is Akar?"

"He is in a foul mood. I sent him back alone to our space. And I did not want Kalli to be around his anger, so Haaka still has her."

"I am going to speak to Artadel. I will come and find you when I am done."

"How many are joining us to open Kthama Minor, do we know?"

Artadel thought. "Twenty perhaps, Haan. Fifteen are males. None of them are Elders, which I understand. They are too old to help significantly and they might not survive it."

"I hope we will gain more numbers before it is time to begin. It is going to take every one of us to do this. And we must begin preparation soon."

"We cannot do that here. I will find a secluded spot," Artadel volunteered. "But you are bringing this up the moment you return. Has something happened?"

"Tarnor. It came to blows. He threatened Hakani, Akar'Tor, even our offling, Kalli. I fear we are on the brink of the Wrak-Ayya." Haan frowned.

"That we must avoid at all costs. Even if we have to leave Kayerm instead of them."

"You have also heard that? It is what Tarnor said, that our numbers are fewer and that we should leave."

"I would consider what he said, Adik'Tar. It does make sense. And in time, their anger will dissipate— and they will have no cause to go after the Akassa. Whereas if we force them out, they will turn on the Akassa in anger."

"So many questions, Artadel. Perhaps the threat of annihilation was not from them; perhaps it was just a logical projection of what would happen if our tribes came to war."

"There are too few of us. We do not have enough numbers to populate a new Sassen line."

"Then, so be it. If this is the end of the Sassen, there is nothing we can do. The Fathers failed in their charge to protect the Others, but we cannot fail the Akassa."

Haan looked up at the stars overhead as he had done so many times. The same stars that his forefathers had looked up at.

So this is the end of us. Within a few generations, Tarnor will be forced to face the truth. But by then, it will be too late. I pray the Sassen will not truly perish from the land. If there are other Sassen out there, I hope they are wiser than we.

"You returned with Akar'Tor."

"Yes. He is in our quarters by now with his mother and sister. I have had to post guards there after Tarnor's threat. And it is not just him. Tarnor has a following; it could be anyone. This is no way to live."

Haan sighed.

"I must consider what Tarnor said. Perhaps we should leave Kayerm. But where are we to go—"

"Once the decision is made, half the journey is begun," said Artadel, quoting the words of the Ancients. "The answer will come."

"I need to sleep. I will await your word about a place where we can begin the preparations."

Haan lay awake for a while. He was exhausted, but his mind still churned. *How many times must I wrestle with this? Did I violate the Rah'hora by bringing Hakani here? Or was bringing her here the only hope for the Akassa? Because they lost the knowledge of Kthama Minor with their Healer's untimely death, had I not made contact, they would never have known of its existence. And their knowledge of their own history is flawed.* He sighed. *I hope they are strong enough to weather the rest of the truth.*

He turned over and put his arm around Hakani. *Despite what I learned about the truth between you and Khon'Tor, I do love you—but I can see you are now unhappy here. I know you are filled with bitterness; it seems you are becoming more and more lost. I do not know what the future holds, but I will do what I can to help you find peace again.*

When Adia returned to their living space that evening, the scent of lavender hit her as soon as she opened the door. Their quarters had been beautifully adorned with flowers and petals, and soft fluorescent stones were placed along the walls.

She found Acaraho waiting for her on their sleeping mat and she smiled, pleased that he had gone to this trouble to create such a beautiful setting.

By the way he was looking at her, she could tell what he had in mind for the evening.

She loosened the front of her wrapping and walked toward him as his eyes hungrily ran up and down her figure.

He extended his hand to help her down next to him, and she started to speak, but he placed his fingers on her lips.

"Sssh. I know we have become consumed with the mechanics of mating, but tonight this is only about you and me and our pleasure together. About enjoying each other as for so many years, we longed to do." And he brought his lips to hers and kissed her softly.

Acaraho had never attended the Ashwea Tare, but with experience, he had learned what pleased her and how to make her long for him to fill her. It was the male's responsibility to bring the female to him, to wait until she was soaked with lust before taking her. Especially with a male of Acaraho's size, if he took Adia without building her desire for him, the taking would be painful.

She wrapped an arm around his neck and leaned in, her breasts brushing against his chest. He reached up and undid her top wrapping, sliding it off onto the mat behind her and returning to softly tease the tips, which he knew would inflame her desire for him. He placed his hand against the back of her neck and pulled her harder into him for a more passionate kiss. He slipped his other hand under her, moving aside the wrapping to caress her soft folds. He knew he was pleasing her as his fingers were soon slick with her response to his touch.

"Ahhmm," Adia moaned. She pulled him tighter to her and lay back, bringing him down to face her. She wrapped her hand around him; he was making no secret of how much he wanted her.

They had no agenda; the night was theirs, and there was nowhere else to be.

Acaraho kept his hand on her, the sounds escaping her lips letting him know his swirls and circles were bringing her close to completion. He resisted the drive to enter her, focusing only on her release for now. She tensed and arched her back. He kept his rhythm steady, knowing she was close, then watched her lose herself to ecstasy as it expanded, peaking for a delicious moment, and then collapsing back on itself in wave after exquisite wave of satisfaction. She moaned and relaxed against him, enjoying the last few waning ripples of pleasure.

He waited until Adia opened her eyes before continuing. Never breaking his gaze, he gently moved over her, rolling her onto her back. He brushed her hair from her forehead with one hand while he positioned himself against her with the other. It was his turn to moan as he pressed himself into her, feeling her yield to him as he entered. He teased them both with short slow strokes, resisting the nearly overpowering drive to bury himself in her as hard and deep as possible. He felt her tense under him as he continued, and she wrapped her legs around his hips, raising her own to meet his thrusts. She balled her fists in the covering over his hips and pulled him harder against her, demanding that he drive himself deeper.

"Yes, please, oh, please!" She begged him to take her harder and faster, but he teased her a while longer before he complied. As she dug her nails into him, he realized that she was at the end of her limits. He reached under her hips and braced her while he buried himself as fully as he could—making her cry out in satisfaction and bringing himself immediately to the point of no return. He felt her tighten around him and knew that she had reached a second splendor, just before he lost himself, pumping the load of his hot seed deep within her.

Exhausted, satisfied, so great was the relief that they laughed as they pulled apart. They turned to face each other on the mat.

"My," Adia said, trying to catch her breath. "When did you learn how to be such a tease, my love? Are you males telling stories in the meeting rooms after the shifts end?" she chuckled.

"You are my inspiration. I realized I have gotten so focused on seeding you that I have forgotten to show you how much I love you. And that you are and will always be the only one for me," he whispered.

"And you for me. How did we get here? From the times where you stood stoically against the wall of my quarters, never saying a word, to the first time you spoke my name and time stopped. All the years of sorrow knowing I was the reason you never paired —knowing I had robbed you of a chance to experience love in the way you deserved, in a way I could never give you. If you only saw the way the other females looked at you. You could have had any one you wanted, yet you stayed by my side—giving up any chance of real happiness for me."

Tears shone in her eyes. "Then, by the grace of the Great Mother, the High Council relented. And here we are. The love of my life beside me. You, who stood by me all those years, protecting me, looking out for me. Asking nothing in return and knowing nothing could ever be given. I do not deserve you or the blessings you have brought me."

Adia turned and buried her face in his chest as the tears fell down her cheeks.

Acaraho wrapped his arms around her, stroking her hair as she released her pain.

"I never regretted a moment, Adia. I knew there would never be anyone for me but you. And if that meant a lifetime of unsatisfied longing, well, that was better than anything I could have had with anyone else. And if we never have offspring of our own, this is enough. This is more than enough. This is more than I ever could have hoped for and all I ever could have dreamed. My only desire is to spend my life with you, and if the day comes that we are parted, I will count every second until we are reunited again in the One."

"Yes, only death can part us, Acaraho. And then but for a while. And after that, we need never be apart again—ever."

The silence of the night descended and wrapped itself around them like a sacred blanket. They stayed in each other's arms, their hearts filled with gratitude for having been given the miracle of each other's love.

The morning found them awake before daylight. Adia stirred first, then turned to cuddle with Acaraho, stretching out their time together just a bit longer.

Acaraho rolled over and sleepily smiled at his mate.

"Sleep well?"

"Better than I have in a long time," he grinned. "Why are you awake; it is not even first light," he pointed out.

"I do not know; I just woke up," she said.

Adia started thinking about what it would be like for her and Acaraho to miss out on offspring of their own. At least they had raised Nootau and Oh'Dar together.

She had often wondered about Acaraho's experiences as an offspring, and now she asked him. "In all these years, we have never spoken about your family. I know nothing of your father or mother.

You never mention them, so I have not wanted to ask."

"That is because your path and mine both had their share of heartache, and I did not want to add to your burden by sharing mine. I know your mother died giving you life, and your father years later, after you had left the Deep Valley community. I never knew my parents. I came to the High Rocks as a very young offling and was raised within Awan's family as one of their own."

Adia propped herself up on one elbow so she could see him.

"That is why you and Awan have such trust?"

"Partly yes; we were raised as brothers. I learned a great deal from his father about character and honesty. He was everything I aspired to be. And I know who Awan has become, so much like his father —which is why I trust him."

"How could I not know this about you?"

"I hardly ever think about it myself. I have never asked for details about my past; I never wanted to know, and I blocked it out. I have always tried to be the best I could be, developing my skills, my character. Hoping that whoever my parents were, if they were still alive, they would somehow know and be proud. There are so many of us; I am just one more who does not talk about the past. When questions are raised, I change the subject. Most people do not pry any further."

"What do you know about your mother and father?"

"Only their names and another name from farther back. And I have my family symbol. Anything else was never shared with me, and I always assumed it was intentional, for my own protection. Do I have a right to know? Perhaps, but I have made peace with it. Sometimes the truth can be detrimental and serves only to punish those who are innocent—those who are not guilty of others' failings, yet must pay the price for them. Whatever the truth is, my life is here. I let the rest of it go a long time ago," he finished.

Adia knew he was not keeping anything from her; she could sense that he was being completely truthful. He no longer felt animosity or real pain about it—it was as it was.

While he was talking, she could not help but think of her choice not to reveal Khon'Tor's attack on her. And her failure as yet to let Nimida and Nootau know they were siblings. *I believe I will struggle with this all of my days. Sometimes the right choice is not clear cut.*

Respecting Acaraho's privacy, she changed the topic. "I need to see Tehya today. Considering the size of the father, I am getting a bit worried about her. She is not showing enough for how far along she is. But the offling is hopefully taking after her and is naturally small. I could not bear it if anything happened to their offspring *again*. The unspoken question is whether Khon'Tor would be able to seed another because counting back, this seeding must have taken hold just before he became sick.

"I wish Oh'Dar were here." Adia fell silent as a cold wave of fear passed through her core. *Oh'Dar has to return in time for Tehya's delivery.*

"What's wrong?" Acaraho frowned, his eyes tracing the lines that furrowed his mate's brow. "You are trembling!"

"I— I have to contact Oh'Dar somehow. He has to come home. Now," she stammered.

Acaraho paused, having learned to trust his mate's premonitions. "In all your learning with Urilla Wuti, is there no way to get a message to him? You pushed a message to me once, as I remember—the one that stopped me from killing Khon'Tor after we thought Hakani had killed herself."

"It was a time of great duress. But you are right. I hate to interrupt Oh'Dar with whatever he is doing, but it would still take him time to get here. He and Tehya are close, and regardless, he would want to be here if there were a problem."

She paused. "If I cannot reach him, I am sure I know someone who can," she said, alluding to Urilla Wuti.

Adia's hands purposefully moved over Tehya's belly. Khon'Tor had placed his mate on the work table—

easily lifting her tiny frame onto the stone slab. There was a stuffed mat there for her comfort—an idea Oh'Dar had come up with while he was last at Kthama.

Khon'Tor stood by Tehya, his hand on her shoulder. Urilla Wuti also stood watching.

When Adia was finished, Urilla Wuti stepped forward. After she completed the same check that Adia had, she asked Tehya, "May I have your permission to do a different kind of examination of your offspring?"

"Of course, Urilla Wuti, you know I trust you."

Khon'Tor frowned.

"It will not hurt. I just need a moment, and you should not feel anything."

The Healer closed her eyes and exhaled. She stood for a moment, her hand resting on Tehya's belly.

Then she raised her head and opened her eyes to look at Tehya.

"There is no problem; she is just naturally tiny."

"She!" exclaimed Adia.

"She?" asked Tehya.

"*She*?" echoed Khon'Tor.

Tehya turned quickly to her mate, tears in her eyes.

"Leave us, please," he ordered, and the others stepped out into the corridor.

Turning to his mate, he asked her, "Why are you crying? She is fine; there is nothing wrong! This is a time for rejoicing, not one for tears."

"You need a son. I have to give you a son," and her voice cracked.

Khon'Tor picked up one of her hands and held it in his while he laid the other gently on her head.

"I need *you*. Anything and everything else is just extra. The tiny offspring is fine. She is just little, like you. That is great news, Tehya. Do not have any regrets. There is more than enough time for you to bear me a son, but it does not matter; I thought you knew that. As long as I have you, I have more than I could have hoped for—or deserve. And to have a little Tehya as well—"

But Tehya's eyes still brimmed with tears, so he continued.

"Before you, the only thing I cared about was being the great Khon'Tor, Leader of the largest community of the People in the region—maybe the greatest Leader across all the lands. None of that matters any longer. I would walk away from everything in a moment if you asked me to, and I would never look back. You must believe me!"

Tehya nodded, the tears leaving wet streaks down the sides of her face. She took his hand and pressed it to her lips.

Khon'Tor turned to Adia. "What special care does Tehya need?"

"She is fine, and so is your daughter. The best thing for them now is rest. Soon you will have a tiny Tehya crawling about your quarters, getting into everything, and making your hearts smile."

Khon'Tor leaned over the table and wrapped his arms around his mate. "Thank you for your help—I am taking her home now." He swept Tehya up, cradled her in his arms, and carried her out past the others.

Khon'Tor carried Tehya down the corridor to their quarters. The guards stationed there opened the wooden door and stepped aside. He carried her in and set her down on their sleeping mat, covering her with one of the large fur pelts. Kweeuu curled up next to her on the mat, and Khon'Tor let him stay.

He went back and closed the wooden door, telling one of the guards to let Acaraho know that he would be in his quarters if needed. Khon'Tor had no intention of leaving Tehya's side while she was still upset.

He stretched out next to her, and she immediately cuddled over to take her favorite spot up against him, her head cradled in the crook of his shoulder.

Before long, someone clacked the announcement stone outside the open doorway

Khon'Tor looked over toward the door. "Come in," he called out.

Mapiya poked her head in and asked if she could enter; she had brought them something to eat. "If she is up to it, there is some calming broth here for

Tehya, sent by Adia." She set everything on the work-table and asked if there was anything else they needed.

"No, thank you, Mapiya, but I appreciate your thoughtfulness."

"If you change your mind, just send word."

Tehya shook her head and buried her face in Khon'Tor's warm chest covering, letting her tears soak into the thick warm curls.

Khon'Tor did not know how to console her, so he held her. Sandwiched between the warmth of her virile mate and the giant grey wolf who lay behind her, it was not long before he could tell by her breathing that Tehya was finally asleep.

Back in the Healer's Quarters, Adia was wondering why Urilla Wuti had revealed the gender of Tehya's offspring.

"I am curious; why did you reveal that the offspring is a female?"

"Tehya is worrying herself sick. She has been around other females who are seeded, and she knows she is not big enough for the age of the offspring. She needed to know it is a female so she can accept that it is natural for it to be this size, considering her build. Yes, normally, we would expect even a female to be larger considering Khon'-Tor's physique—but it seems the offspring is going to favor her mother greatly. The second reason is that Tehya was worrying so much that she would not be producing a son for Khon'Tor. That needed to come out in the open and sooner, rather than later. Khon'Tor could not have risen to the occasion more perfectly. He speaks the truth—he truly does not care about anything but her. He has changed significantly from the one who—"

"Hopefully, now she will calm down and enjoy this precious time. With Akar'Tor gone, maybe Khon'Tor will also relax," said Adia.

"Let us visit her tomorrow if she is up to it," said Nadiwani. " Perhaps she needs some female comfort now. Will you come with us, Urilla Wuti? We could take some of Pakuna's designs for her to go over; I think that would cheer her up."

"I will be glad to come."

"I cannot wait," exclaimed Nadiwani, heading for the door. "I will tell Pakuna, Mapiya, and Nimida too. We could meet after the first meal, perhaps?"

"Yes; maybe we can help her name her daughter."

When they were alone, the energy in the room shifted, and Adia spoke, "Urilla Wuti, I need your help. Oh'Dar must return home. I know he just left, but I have a terrible feeling that I cannot shake; he *must* be here before Tehya delivers."

"My Connection with him is clearer than yours; remember we set it up that way on purpose? I will be glad to send him a message."

"I hate to pull him away from Shadow Ridge. If I could shake this, I would," Adia said.

"You know better than to ignore your seventh sense, Adia. If you feel he needs to be here, then he does. If anything were to go wrong, you would never forgive yourself if you ignored a warning."

Adia nodded and agreed, grateful for Urilla Wuti's help.

CHAPTER 6

Oh'Dar brought Lightning up to a slow stop in front of the stables. Jenkins was right behind him on Storm. The morning ride had been exhilarating for both riders and their steeds.

Oh'Dar swung his leg up and over and jumped down. After Jenkins dismounted, they led the stallions into the stalls to be groomed.

"I think Lightning is as fast as Storm, do you agree?" asked Oh'Dar.

"I think you're right, son, though I'd never have believed that any other sire could produce a line to rival Dreamer's." He paused in reflection. "What shall we study today, Grayson? Would you like to work more on how to breed for composition and temperament?"

"I think I understand the elements of composition, so let's focus on temperament. I already understand that the best composition in the world won't make up for a surly animal," Oh'Dar said.

"These are powerful beasts, and you're correct. But, just as with composition, some traits of temperament are dominant and have to be factored into the combination."

Oh'Dar stopped for a moment. A strange feeling came over him. In his mind, he could see Tehya. She was standing in a field, the wind blowing through her long hair. Her gauzy wrappings were twisting in the breeze, and the sunlight behind her clearly showed she was carrying an offspring. There was no feeling of alarm. He shook his head to clear the vision, lest Jenkins wonder what had come over him.

Later that evening, as he was lying in bed waiting to go to sleep, it came again. This time she was laughing somewhere, maybe his workshop. His mother was there with Nadiwani. Again, there was no sense of alarm, but again, he could see she was seeded.

What are you telling me? Clearly, Tehya is seeded. But what do you want me to do?

Oh'Dar lay there a while, and then the first vision appeared again, only this time, off on the horizon, dark storm clouds were alarmingly gathering. He thought back to the times he and Tehya had spent in his workshop, laughing about her ideas and going through the hides and materials. He remembered how sick she had been when the illness swept through Kthama and how worried they all were, especially Khon'Tor. Oh'Dar remembered how the Leader had turned to him again and again for advice, and how his mother had said that Khon'Tor had looked to him for input even more than he looked to Adia. And how devastating it had been when Tehya lost her offspring from the sickness.

Suddenly Oh'Dar figured it out. They were a message. In both visions, he could tell that Tehya was not in distress. But in the second one, storm clouds were gathering and drawing very close.

Tehya is seeded again. Everything is alright at the moment, but something is going to go wrong. As he lay there, he realized he had to return to Kthama quickly. He loved being at Shadow Ridge with his grandmother and Jenkins. But Oh'Dar knew where he had to be.

He had to go *home*.

The next morning at breakfast, Oh'Dar watched them casually enjoying the lavish meal Mrs. Thomas had prepared. His grandmother and Jenkins were lost in their enjoyment of warm biscuits, sweet fresh jams, berry preserves, and thick warm butter, the smells of which filled the eating area. He had to admit he'd developed a taste for the rich Waschini foods. It would be hard to go back to a diet of vegetables, berries, roots, and raw meat after this.

Life at Shadow Ridge was pleasant. Jenkins had

become part father, part friend to him. Oh'Dar could talk to him about anything—except the very thing that mattered most. Between his apprenticeship with Dr. Miller and what Jenkins was teaching him, Oh'Dar felt he'd be taking usable knowledge back to Kthama. He didn't claim to know all that Jenkins or Dr. Miller knew—not by any means—but his confidence was growing that what he'd learned would somehow play a role in helping the People.

However, as pleasant as life at Shadow Ridge was, he realized that it lacked a feeling of purpose and a sense of fulfillment. Even without the premonition, his life at Kthama was beckoning him to return.

That night, Oh'Dar went down to the ranch hands' quarters and joined Jenkins and the others sitting around a late evening fire. The men started to stand as he approached, but he motioned them back down. He'd become friends with several, one of whom was Mrs. Thomas' oldest boy, Zeke.

"May I join you, gentlemen?" he asked.

They made a place for him on the logs surrounding the fire pit. Overhead, the night sky was ablaze with stars.

One of the men, Mrs. Thomas' boy, had a harmonica, and the lonesome tunes fascinated Oh'Dar. *Perhaps I should buy one of those for Tehya— maybe her offspring would like the sounds it makes.*

Thanks to Grandmother's stipend, I've more money than I know what to do with.

As the evening passed, the men sat mostly in silence, occasionally trading stories, until eventually only he and Jenkins were left by the fire.

Oh'Dar looked up at the Milky Way stretched across the night sky.

"What do you think is out there, Ben?" he asked. "Do you think there are other worlds, places that we know nothing about?"

"I don't know that I've ever thought about that, Grayson. But I suppose so. I certainly don't think we know everything there is to know."

"What about here? On Mother Eter—on Mother Earth? Do you believe there are mysteries here that people have no idea about?"

"I've no doubt. But whatever they are, I hope they remain a secret. From what I've seen of our kind, we seem to destroy everything we don't understand."

Oh'Dar frowned, surprised at what Jenkins was saying. It sounded like something the People would say of the Waschini. To hear Jenkins use virtually the same words took him aback. "Why do you say that?"

"Oh, don't mind me, Grayson. I'm just getting old and cynical. I've seen too much of life and miss the spark I used to have for living. I love your grandmother, and we have a comfortable life, a profitable business, and reliable, trusted work hands. And you couldn't ask for a better person than Mrs. Thomas to look after us all. But the routine at the ranch is getting mundane with Zeke and his brother having taken over most of my duties running the place, which does free me up to spend more time with you teaching you about breeding. But in truth, I could use some of that mystery you talk about."

I could tell you of wonders you wouldn't believe, and how I wish it were possible. This is my greatest torment, belonging to two worlds, which are, by their nature, incompatible. How I wish I could take you and Grandmother back with me to Kthama. I wonder, could your minds handle it? Could mine—had I not grown up in that world? What would you think, standing in the Great Entrance at Kthama, staring at the magnificent giants that are the People? Finding out that there's an entirely different way of living than you could ever imagine?

Oh'Dar put his hands on his knees, ready to get up. "I'm going to turn in. Thank you for letting me join you."

"You're always welcome, son."

Oh'Dar stepped a few feet away, then stopped and turned back, "Ben, what if I told you—" He stopped before continuing. "No—never mind. Good night."

Jenkins smothered the fire and headed for the house too. As he slipped into bed with his bride, he was pleased to see she was still awake, reading.

"Something happened tonight, Viv," he said.

She peered at him over her reading glasses, then seeing the serious look on her face, folded her book, and placed it on the nightstand.

"What is it, Ben?"

"Grayson. He joined us tonight down at the evening fire. It's a quiet night, and the stars are brighter than ever. Zeke played his harmonica as he often does. Then, after the others turned in and it was just the two of us, I had the distinct impression he was about to tell me something—significant. Something about his past. Something perhaps even —unbelievable."

"Unbelievable? What do you mean?"

"I don't know. It was just how he was talking—as if he wanted to confide in me, but it was too much to expect me to understand or accept." He sighed.

"I'm not going to press him," Jenkins continued. "If he wants to tell me, he will, but he has me wondering now. If you could have heard how he talked. Almost—there was almost a magical quality to what he was suggesting."

"Grayson is a mystery himself," answered Miss Vivian. "Perhaps he'll always be. It must be hard on him to keep whatever secrets he holds. I believe he's happy here, but it's also clear he's still torn by thoughts of whatever his life was before he came to us."

"He certainly has grown. He looks more like his father every day. The last time I rode into town with him to pick up some supplies, I stopped by Dr.

Miller's. His new assistant is pretty taken with Grayson. She's a cute little thing, blonde hair, long lashes. She was doing everything but standing on her head to get him to notice her."

"Did he?" she asked.

"Not for a second. I swear the boy is the most dedicated soul I've ever met. He's all about learning —from Dr. Miller, from me, from the hands, even from Mrs. Thomas! He soaks up everything you can throw at him. Whatever he's bound for, his mind is focused on it like a steel trap. Anyone who can ignore a pretty little blonde like that must have a commitment burning inside him, driving him to something far greater than most of us can imagine."

"Oh, fiddle-sticks," she said.

Jenkins chuckled. He put his arm around her and pulled her close to him.

"I know, I know. You want Grayson to get married and fill Shadow Ridge with grandchildren. But I just don't know if that's on the cards for him—or us."

She cuddled in, and Ben reached over and turned down the lamp, so only the moonlight coming through the lace curtains lit the room.

As his bride drifted off to sleep in his arms, Ben wondered again what mysteries Grayson had been about to confide.

Oh'Dar lay awake in his room. *I almost told Ben about the People. I wanted to tell him something; I'm not even sure what. Maybe one can't understand it in words. They think the Brothers raised me, and I should leave it at that. I'm looking for a way to join the two halves of my life when there isn't one.*

He rolled over and faced the window, the soft moonlight reminding him that his people were looking up at the same night skies over Kthama. The breeze coming in brought scents of the recent rain, the richness of the acres and acres of fields and woods that made up Shadow Ridge.

I must let Mama know I'm coming home. He chuckled out loud to himself, alone in his room. He knew the situation was serious, but a funny thought came to him. *Urilla Wuti made a stirring between Kweeuu and me. I wonder if I could get a message to her through him. I'm going to try.*

Oh'Dar remembered how Urilla Wuti had him quiet his mind, clear his thoughts before she created the stirring. He did the same and focused on Kweeuu. He tried to push a visual image to the wolf, thinking perhaps that was how he'd received the visions of Tehya.

When he finished, he pulled the covers up over him. *Even though Tehya isn't really part of my family, in every way that matters, she's like a sister to me. After losing her first offspring from the sickness, now she's seeded again, and for some reason, I'm needed there. With all my heart, I know my place is with her. Even though it'll disappoint Grandmother terribly, I have to leave Shadow Ridge.*

Finally, Oh'Dar drifted off to sleep.

He woke with worries already on his mind about how to tell his grandmother that he was leaving again. Oh'Dar wished he could explain to her about Tehya and how they needed him there. *Perhaps I can; they'll assume I'm talking about the Brothers. I can tell them some things without telling them the crucial details that would make it unbelievable. They do know where my parents were killed, but there's no real way they could find Kthama from there, and especially if they don't know to look for it. And no Waschini could imagine the truth of my past.*

He immediately felt better, realizing that he could give them a reason for his need to return.

"Good Morning!" he greeted them with a lighter heart than he'd turned in with the night before.

Jenkins looked over at his wife and raised an eyebrow.

"You seem in a good mood this morning, Grayson."

"I had a lot on my mind last night, sorry, Ben," he apologized.

"No need to apologize. Have some gravy on those biscuits."

"I'm going to miss this!" Oh'Dar blurted out.

Then he stopped, looking up to see they'd both paused what they were doing in mid-motion.

"I'm sorry. I didn't mean it like that. No, I have to explain something. Maybe this will make it easier. Yes, I have to go back for a while. I know I haven't told you anything about my past, but I can tell you this. There's a friend of mine; she's pregnant with her first child. And where she is, well, they'd feel better if I were with her for this. It's hard on you, my coming and going; I know this. But she needs me now, and I have to go. I wish I could take you both with me—" and his voice drifted off.

They looked at each other. Miss Vivian's cup clinked as she set it down on the saucer.

"We understand, Grayson. I think Ben and I have both made peace with this part of your life—as long as you always come back. I'd be broken-hearted never to see you again," she admitted.

"Grayson," she continued, her voice soft, "where you were—did you have another name? I always wanted to ask you that."

Oh'Dar thought for a while before answering, considering if there was anything about his name that would sound—*otherworldly* was the only term he could think of.

"I was called Oh'Dar."

After he said it out loud, he realized it sounded like one of the Brothers' names. *Come to think of it, so many of our names flow like theirs—Is'Taqa, Acaraho,*

Ithua, Nadiwani—and then there are the harder-sounding ones—Kahrok, Kurak'Kahn.

"Thank you for sharing that. I'm sure being called Grayson Morgan Stone the Third sounded peculiar to you," she said.

"It did. But I've gotten used to it. It's as if I'm two people, Grandmother. Two people belonging to two impossibly different worlds—"

"Let me know when you're getting ready to leave and what you need for your trip. You're welcome to take Storm again if you wish," offered Jenkins.

"I'd love to take Storm, yes." Then he had an idea, "Would you mind, if Storm bred with other horses? They'd never be competition to Shadow Ridge."

"I don't care provided your grandmother doesn't."

"If it'll help your other family—please, feel free. But remember, a stallion can easily become unruly around mares who are ready to breed."

"I know. I'll be careful, I promise." *I don't know if the Brothers would even be interested, but it would certainly improve their stock if we could get some of Dreamer's bloodline into them! At least I have permission.*

Oh'Dar was packed and ready to leave within days. He had a full supply of food for the trip. Without Kweeuu to worry about, he could ride openly for most of the distance. He'd packed his water canteens and his travel clothes, which he'd change into when he got close to the Brothers' village. Until then, he was a Waschini traveler crossing the changing countryside on a magnificent stallion.

Knowing he had the blessing of both his grandmother and Jenkins made this trip different from the last time. *Since I don't have Kweeuu with me, I might be able to stop and see Mrs. Webb and Grace this time. I have to stop and let Storm rest anyway.*

Oh'Dar made sure to remember the red jasper necklace he'd made for his mother—the one Adia had placed around his neck before he left as a promise of his return. And the beautifully polished wooden combs, like the one Honovi had, which he'd bought for the other females—his mother, Ithua, Nadiwani, Tehya, Acise and her sister—with a few extra just in case. For Honovi, he'd bought a beautiful brocade pouch to keep her comb in, since she already had one. He'd also bought something else for Honovi that he knew all the women of the Brothers would love and would most likely be shared—a looking glass with a smoothly polished dark wooden handle. And for the males he had the Waschini knives, though Is'Taqa would have to decide if Noshoba was old enough to have his yet.

While Oh'Dar was preparing to leave, Jenkins tucked his pistol into one of the saddlebags, as he'd done before.

"Just in case, son. You never know."

Oh'Dar did not want that weapon. It was a burden to store safely and secretly at Kthama. Luckily, the People did not enter another's quarters uninvited, let alone go through personal belongings, and he'd long ago hollowed out a place in the rock wall for the pistol, using one of the larger storage baskets to cover it up.

They've no idea how well I can defend myself with a bow and arrow, and how much I prefer it. When I return to Shadow Ridge, I'll show Ben how to make the perfect set and convince him that I don't need this Waschini weapon. But for now, he let it go, knowing it comforted them that he had it.

Then Oh'Dar mounted Storm, waved goodbye, and left Shadow Ridge once again.

As he rode off, Jenkins turned to Miss Vivian and said, "I have just two questions. One, of course, is when will he return? And the second is, *how in the world did he know his friend was pregnant?*"

Adia, Nadiwani, and the other females were enjoying their time in Oh'Dar's workshop. Pakuna laid out sketches of new designs—on which she had tried to copy some of the flourishes that Oh'Dar had always incorporated. The females were going over them, all now excited at the prospect of new wrappings. Even Urilla Wuti was interested.

"Tehya, you have inspired us!" laughed Nimida.

"Once we all decide, we can start cutting the patterns," suggested Tehya. "There is more than enough material here for us all. I do not know how it got here but—"

"Acaraho brought it from the Brothers' village. Oh'Dar and Is'Taqa spent the last summer he was there trapping and preparing the skins," Adia explained.

At the mention of Oh'Dar's name, Kweeuu suddenly got up and went to a far corner of the workshop. When he came back, he had the bear that Oh'Dar had made for him out of hide. As a cub. Kweeuu was caught playing with the stuffed bear that Adia had found with the abandoned Oh'Dar and had almost torn it up. That was when Oh'Dar made Kweeuu one of his own out of the toughest hide available.

Adia and Urilla Wuti looked down at the giant grey wolf standing in front of them, wagging his tail with the hide bear in his mouth.

"He has not touched that toy since Oh'Dar left," said Nadiwani.

Kweeuu dropped the toy at Urilla Wuti's feet.

The older Healer looked up at Adia and smiled.

"Oh'Dar is on his way home," she said.

"Oh," exclaimed Tehya. "How do you know? Are you sure?"

"Yes, I am sure, Tehya. It will be a little while before he gets here, but he will arrive before you have your offspring."

Impulsively, Tehya and Adia hugged each other.

Then the Healer asked, "Have you thought of any names for your offspring?"

"Well, now that I know it is a she—"

"A female!" Pakuna and Nimida squealed with delight. "Oh, what fun! We can make an assortment of little wrappings for her."

"That is a great idea. She will need wrappings, so why should they not be cute? If she takes after me, she will find Kthama cooler than the other offspring do."

"Wait," said Nimida. "How do you know it is a female?"

"Urilla Wuti told me," was all Tehya offered, smiling.

"Ah," replied Nimida, knowing that Healers had ways of knowing things.

Adia's mind was racing. *Urilla Wuti's message got through, and Oh'Dar is coming home. Acaraho and Khon'Tor will also be glad to hear he is on his way back. I wonder if he will get here before Haan returns to open Kthama Minor?*

She could not wait to tell Acaraho and Nootau.

Haan and Artadel stood with the small group of those who had pledged to open Kthama Minor and help the Akassa. There were thirty-nine who stood with him now. Haan hoped it would be enough.

They were not as powerful as those who would have sealed Kthama Minor. It would probably take all their strength and preparation to break the seal and open it again.

Artadel had found a secluded area for their use. Supplies were being put in place, and those who were not directly participating would guard the others. Their families were also getting ready for their absence.

When it was time, they would stay in this sacred location for several days, weeks even—as long as it took until they were purified and connected and could move as one. One body, one soul, one consciousness, one intention. This joining had not been accomplished since the time of the Mothoc. It was an ancient ritual and called into use only under the direst of times. Until they achieved unity, they would not leave the area. And once it was achieved, they would have no separate, individual consciousness until their mission was completed.

Back at Kayerm, Hakani and the other females were unsure of what was going on. She was worried, though Haan had tried to explain it to her. He was going to be gone for an unknown period and had left his most trusted guards to protect them. But now Akar'Tor had taken to disappearing during the day, returning only just before twilight. He never told her where he went or what he did. At first, she feared he had returned to Kthama, but as he came back each evening, she knew that was impossible.

One evening she pinned Akar'Tor down. "Where do you go? What are you up to? I am worried about you."

"Do not worry about me, Mother. I am fine. I have a project I am working on, that is all. It keeps me out of your way, though I will be finished soon," he tried to reassure his mother.

Hakani was not reassured. With Haan away, she did not like Akar'Tor leaving too; and she feared that what he was doing had something to do with his anger with Khon'Tor. At least she had Haaka's company every day. They passed the time weaving baskets and taking care of Kalli.

"You do love Kalli, do you not?" Hakani said to Haaka one day.

"Yes, I do. I know she looks more like the Akassa than us, but that makes me more protective of her. I have not yet had offling. I think of her as my adopted daughter. I hope you do not mind that," she added.

Hakani had noticed Haaka looking Haan over. By Sarnonn standards, Hakani knew he was attractive—plus he was the Adik'Tar. She had thought of asking Haan if he wanted to choose Haaka as a second mate. It would take the pressure off of Hakani, even though he had said he would not ask her to mate with him again.

"No, I do not mind, Haaka. I feel close to you, and I am glad you feel that way about Kalli."

Hakani watched her daughter sleep. The dark

cloud in her mind had again lifted momentarily, and she wondered if this was the future of the People. *Is this what will become of us—no longer the People and no longer the Sassen? I am no better off than Akar or Kalli. I have no real place I belong to either. We are all Outsiders in our own ways, and I wish things would return to normal. I wish I could forget about Khon'Tor, that mate of his, and Kthama. I wish Akar and I could find peace here again.*

Haan returned from visiting the site Artadel had selected. He brought Hakani fresh berries he had stopped and picked along the way. Hakani split them between herself and Haaka and thanked Haan for thinking of them.

"The site is almost ready. Now, we wait."

"Wait for what?" Hakani asked as she enjoyed the ripe, beady red fruit.

"A sign. A sign that it is time to begin. I do not know what it will be, but I expect I will know it when it comes."

Hakani waited a moment before bringing up the subject of Akar'Tor. "He has been leaving each day, returning just before nightfall. I do not know where he goes. He says he is working on a project."

Haan sighed. Once he entered the ritual, he would not be able to disengage. He needed Akar'Tor to behave because if trouble developed, he would not be able to help his son or Hakani.

"I will talk to him. I do not know at what time I will be called to this purpose, Hakani. But I will make sure you have enough help and protection while I am away."

Hakani nodded, though her heart was troubled. She did not understand what Haan and his followers were doing. He only said that it was a deep, ancient ritual that had not been practiced for ages. Too much was changing. She found herself regretting her fights with Khon'Tor. She wished she could go back and do it all over again. That she could take a different tack, find a way to make peace with being Second Choice, and still have the comfort and community of Kthama —still be Third Rank. She hated that her anger continued to flare at Khon'Tor, however much he deserved it, and that she could not control her jealousy of his new mate. More than anything, she wished she could have a second chance at a life of peace and belonging. But at this moment, when the dark clouds that muddled her thinking were abated, in her heart, she knew that it would never be—she had caused too much damage and hurt too many. Whatever her fate was, she was certain that it would not be amid the comfort and familiarity of Kthama's protective walls.

CHAPTER 7

Oh'Dar and Storm made good time crossing the huge expanse that separated Shadow Ridge from the Brothers' territory. The weather cooperated, and he enjoyed the solace of the journey, moving as one with the beautiful stallion.

He bedded down at night under the starlit sky, wondering what his mother and father were doing and if they understood the message he'd sent through Kweeuu. He ran his mind over the gifts he'd brought for the women. For his father, Khon'Tor, Chief Ogima, Is'Taqa, Nootau, and Noshoba, there were the special knives, like nothing they would have seen before, with edges sharper than either the Brothers or the People could hone. Though they had little need for weapons, he knew they'd appreciate the workmanship. *I should have bought one of those*

harmonicas for Noshoba, but I'm giving his father one of
the knives to keep for when he's old enough.

The days passed, and Oh'Dar knew he was nearing
the village where Mrs. Webb and her daughter Grace
had found him. There was no reason to bypass it. He
didn't have Kweeuu to worry about, and he knew that
he had to stop and let Storm rest off and on anyway. He
turned Storm and wound down the hillside and
through the winding streets until he found their house.

Oh'Dar dismounted and tied Storm to the front
fence. He peered around the house but didn't see
anyone outside. He was going to call out but then
realized they didn't know he could speak! As he
started up the steps, he heard barking inside the
house. Then the door opened, and a little furry blur
shot out and launched itself into his arms.

"Mama! He's here! Grayson is here!" shouted
Grace through the open door, then scampered back
inside. Mrs. Webb came out and down the stairs with
her daughter. Both ran up and together embraced
Oh'Dar as he held the wriggling dog.

"Oh my, look at you! Look how you've grown.
And how handsome you've become. My goodness,
your new life becomes you," Mrs. Webb said,
beaming at him.

"Thank you, Ma'am," he said, tipping the black
leather hat that everyone said suited him so well.
And both Nora and Grace's mouths hung open.

"You can talk," and they laughed.

"Yes, I can. I wanted to stop by and see you, and thank you for your kindness. You took me in and made me feel welcome. I'll never forget it," he said, still holding Buster, who was furiously licking his neck.

"Buster remembers you," exclaimed Grace, reaching up to pet the dog who was still in Oh'Dar's arms.

"And I remember him. He was a great comfort to me. You all were."

"Oh, do come in. Can you stay for dinner? Perhaps for the night?" Mrs. Webb asked. "I know Mr. Webb and Ned would hate hearing they'd missed you."

"Mama, may he have his old room and sleep with Buster?" Grace looked up at her mother, throwing the idea in to sweeten the deal.

"Yes, of course," said Mrs. Webb. "Please stay, Grayson."

"I'd be glad to. Let me get my bags and take care of Storm, and I'll be right in."

By the time Oh'Dar had groomed and settled Storm in the Webbs' barn, they had dinner waiting on the table. Mr. Webb and Ned had returned from town. They were surprised to see him and even more surprised that he could speak. They all spent the meal exchanging stories of what had happened since they'd last seen each other. Mr. Webb had noticed the gorgeous stallion in the barn and had a barrage of questions once he learned of the breeding program at Shadow Ridge.

"Grayson," began Ned.

Oh'Dar braced himself, knowing the question that was coming next—one he'd avoided all evening.

"All the time you were growing up—when you were missing—where were you?"

Oh'Dar set down his fork and wiped his mouth with the napkin.

"I know you're all curious, and I know you mean no harm in asking. But if I told you, it would create problems for those who took me in and loved and raised me. I hope you can understand that I can't speak of it. It would be a terrible betrayal of those who were there for me when I needed them most."

"I understand," said Ned.

Mrs. Webb let a sigh of disappointment escape. *It isn't such a mystery, though,* she thought to herself. *Even though he does not want to say, there's only one answer, and it's that the locals took him in and raised him. Or, if not those we know about, another group elsewhere.*

"Forgive us for being curious, Grayson. We didn't mean to pry," she said.

"It's natural to want to know. I've had the same issue with my grandmother and those at Shadow Ridge. I understand the curiosity, and I'm sorry I can't satisfy it for you," apologized Oh'Dar.

Before long, the evening had passed, and Oh'Dar

retired to the same room in which he'd spent those first uneasy nights.

Lying on the familiar bed, looking out at the moonlight through the delicate curtains that fluttered in the open window, his mind went over the journey of discovery that his life had become. He was glad he'd left Kthama. If he'd never found his Waschini family, a part of his soul would never have felt settled. More questions had been answered than raised, the most important one being the real definition of family and belonging. Oh'Dar closed his eyes and enjoyed the fresh night air, the soft mattress, and the warmth of little Buster's body curled up against the small of his back.

The next morning he was on his way, though he promised to stop by any time he came through. As Mrs. Webb watched him ride away, she couldn't help but notice again what a handsome man he'd grown into and wished that Grace was just a little bit older.

Honovi and Ithua were busy picking berries when they heard the approaching hoofbeats. The moment they saw the grey coat of the stallion emerging through the brush, they knew it was Oh'Dar returning. They quickly set the berries on the ground and rushed to greet him.

Oh'Dar swung his leg over Storm, dismounted, and embraced them both at once.

"What a wonderful surprise. We are so glad you are back. You look so handsome in those clothes!" The females patted, complemented, and fussed over him until he could take it no longer.

"Stop. Stop, you are embarrassing me," he laughed.

"I had forgotten how blue your eyes are. I swear they grow bluer every time I see you," remarked Honovi.

"Where is Is'Taqa? I brought presents," said Oh'Dar.

"He will be back by nightfall. Come into the village. Everyone will be so pleased to see you."

Everyone, he thought. He realized he was moments from seeing Acise. *What will she think of my return? Has she forgotten about me?* He suddenly realized his throat was dry, and his hands were sweating.

They walked the rest of the way, Storm following along behind them.

As they entered the village, the children ran up to greet them. Oh'Dar tried to keep his attention on them as he greeted each one, resisting the urge to look around for Acise.

However, within a few moments, Acise came out from her parents' dwelling. She stopped a few feet outside, looking over to see what the commotion was about and froze when she recognized Oh'Dar. She turned around and went back into the dwelling, leaving him stunned and confused.

"I should have told you," said Honovi. "Acise is promised to one of the braves."

Oh'Dar could only stare. He had just then realized how much she meant to him. His heart sank, but he wrapped self-control around himself like protective armor.

"I see."

"I am sorry. I had hoped you two would be bonded. I know your mother did too," said Honovi.

"I—" he did not know what to say.

Honovi put her hand on his arm. "I wish I could have warned you."

"It is my fault. I cannot blame Acise. She made it clear she cared for me, and I left her with no hope. At the time, I did not know what I wanted; now I do, but it is too late," he said quietly, looking at where she had been standing.

He forced his gaze away. "I do not know that I can stay now, Honovi. I need some time. Please give my apologies to Is'Taqa. I will return."

"Give my best to your mother and Acaraho," said Ithua.

Oh'Dar mounted Storm and turned the stallion toward Kthama. From inside the dwelling, Acise watched him ride away.

Oh'Dar let Storm run as hard as he wanted once they got to the valley. The wind biting his face helped him hold himself together. He had come all this way to find out he was too late. *It is not her fault; what did I expect? It was unreasonable for me to think she would wait, especially after how I treated her, and not knowing when, if ever, I would return.* But all the logic in the world did nothing to console him. Oh'Dar was heartbroken.

He was close enough to Kthama to make it well before everyone was asleep. But he wasn't ready. He stopped at one of his favorite spots along the Great River and prepared a place to spend the night. Storm enjoyed the cold, shallow water and the grasses at the river's edge. It was a cool evening, but the hard frost had not come yet.

Oh'Dar pulled the saddle off Storm and spread the blanket out on the ground. Then he lay down and stretched out, looking up at the stars and wondering at the order of things. Was there a purpose for his life? Were the pieces falling together as they should? He finally admitted to himself how much he had been looking forward to seeing Acise. That in realizing this was where he belonged, he had also realized that she was the one for him. They had shared a special bond since their youngest years, and their connection had only grown stronger the last time he was at Kthama. But because of his confusion, he had lost her. She had moved on. Now he must also somehow find a way to do so.

But move on to where? To whom? There was no one he was interested in but her. He remembered the kiss they had shared, how light she had been when he carried her to the mat in his workshop. How her hair smelled, the softness of her skin. Their long conversations, how smart she was, and how he enjoyed her company. The thought of her sharing her life with someone else tore him apart. There, alone in the dark, he let his heart break the rest of the way.

The next morning, Oh'Dar pulled his travel wrappings from the saddlebag and changed out of his Waschini clothes. He forced the hated Waschini boots as far down to the bottom of the bag as possible, wishing never to wear them again. He knew he did not *have* to change out of his Waschini outfit, but it would help him transition back to his life with the People.

The watchers would already have notified the People of his approach, probably as early as when he entered the Brothers' village, so he was not surprised that his family was assembled and waiting for him. Oh'Dar was pleased to see Nimida there as well.

The moment he dismounted, he was surrounded and greeted with hugs, laughter, and smiles.

At the back, also waiting to welcome him home were Khon'Tor, Tehya, and Urilla Wuti. When he finished with his family, he went to greet them too.

"I am glad you are back home, Oh'Dar," said Khon'Tor.

"So am I, Adik'Tar. Hello, Urilla Wuti. I am pleased you are here at Kthama," he replied.

Urilla Wuti smiled at him and placed her hand on the side of his face; her eyes crinkled with kindness.

Then Oh'Dar turned his attention to little Tehya, bending down to give her a gentle hug. She was far enough along that it was clear she was seeded, but he did not want to mention it outright. "I see you have new wrappings. And new designs," Oh'Dar remarked, his eyes looking over her warm buckskin coverings. She even had fur coverings fashioned for her feet.

"Yes. I have been using your workshop as you said I could—with some of my friends."

"I am so glad. I will replenish whatever you have used so you will not run out."

"You seem like you have put on some weight," teased Tehya, her eyes twinkling.

Oh'Dar grinned, "I could say the same of you."

She laughed, "Yes, but I have a good excuse. I am carrying Khon'Tor's offspring."

Oh'Dar hugged her again. "I am so happy for you both. When are you due?"

"You got here just in time. I have only a little while to go."

Then Tehya got quiet. "It is a female, Oh'Dar."

Oh'Dar just smiled all the more. "That is wonderful. Etera can always use another tiny blessing such as you."

Tehya's eyes filled with gratitude at his kind words.

Then Kweeuu pushed between Tehya and Khon'Tor to get his turn. He broke out of his training and jumped up at Oh'Dar, who, this time, did not correct him but instead enjoyed the warm embrace. Oh'Dar buried his face in the giant grey wolf's fur and sighed. *I am home.*

"Much has happened. Let us get you settled; then we can all catch up. I assume you will be staying in your workshop?" said Adia.

"It sounds like a band of rogue females has taken it over," he joked. "Perhaps I can stay with Nadiwani and Nootau," he suggested.

"That would be fine with us," Nadiwani answered for them both. "Except Nootau now has his own place. But you and he are welcome to stay over if you wish. There is more than enough room for your sleeping mats, and we've lots to talk about."

As they watched Oh'Dar, Nootau, Nadiwani, and Nimida talking, Acaraho said to Adia, "If he is giving up his workshop as his personal space, and if he plans to stay for a while, perhaps it is time for him to have his own quarters. After all, Nootau moved out some time ago, though I know he is still close to Nadiwani. Due to the sickness and those we lost, we have the extra spaces; Oh'Dar is grown now—and it might induce him to stay. Hopefully, he will take a mate."

Adia watched as her Waschini son excused

himself to get his bags off Storm and released the stallion to the care of the guards for a few moments. "Let me put these away, and I will come back and take care of the horse," Oh'Dar told them.

After he had left, Adia remarked to Acaraho, "He made no mention of stopping to see Is'Taqa and Honovi."

"But the watchers said he did, and we both still have hopes that he and Acise will pair," replied her mate.

With mixed emotions playing over his face, Khon'Tor watched Tehya join Nootau, Nimida, and Nadiwani. He then walked over with Urilla Wuti to join Acaraho and Adia.

"I am sure you are happy he is back. I am glad for Tehya's sake as well. They somehow became close in a very short period," said Khon'Tor.

"I think it is easy to become protective of Tehya. She has an innocence and delicacy that makes you want to take care of her," said Adia.

Acaraho put his arm around Adia's waist. "Let us give them their time together. We can catch up with him later."

"Oh'Dar will not let anything happen to her, Khon'Tor. Akar'Tor is gone; I think it is alright to let her spend time with her friends," said Adia, seeing the look on his face.

Khon'Tor said nothing. *I know I am over-protective of her, but I have no idea how not to be. I am always uncomfortable when she is out of sight. Though I am glad*

Oh'Dar has returned, and I know he would do his best not to let any harm come to her, he is a Waschini. No match for Akar'Tor. I realize that Nootau is there, but I still wish I could lock her away from everything and everyone.

Acaraho caught Oh'Dar's eye and signed that he and Adia would find him later.

"You know that Mother is dying to ask you how long you are staying, Brother," said Nootau, watching their parents walk away. "And probably Father, too."

"I am not going back anytime soon; at least I am not planning on it."

The others waited for Oh'Dar until he had finished taking care of Storm. By the time he got back, they were full of questions.

"What is it like where you go?" asked Nimida.

"So, so different. They live nothing like we do. The Waschini are far more dependent on unnatural things. They seem always to be in a hurry; they have a far stronger drive to—how can I say it—change everything. They see an open plain and wonder how many villages they can build there. They trap and imprison animals for their own uses and think nothing of it. And they use a system of barter based on metals. They are not without flaws, but they are also not the monsters we have been told. They pray, for one thing, though they use different words."

"What are metals, Oh'Dar? asked Nadiwani.

"Ah, metals. Do you remember the locket that Mother found with me? That is made out of metal. It is complicated to create, but many of their tools and household items are made of it."

"And where do they live? What are their dwellings like; are they like those of the Brothers?" she asked again. Nadiwani had missed out on the information that Oh'Dar had shared during his previous visit to Kthama.

"Their homes are made of wood planks cut from trees and fastened together. They are all upright with harsh angles. But there is a lot of difference in how some live compared to others. The first place I stayed in was simple and plain. But Shadow Ridge, my Waschini family's home, is very confusing inside. I thought at first that there might be something wrong with their eyesight because they combine patterns and colors that make your eyes cross. They appear to be more comfortable with what they make out of nature than with nature itself. As I said, they seem driven to modify everything into something other than its natural state. But their food! Oh! There is nothing like it—*that* I will miss!"

"Please make us some Wachini food someday!" exclaimed Tehya.

"Maybe. I will see if I can figure out how to duplicate their ingredients," he answered.

"Tell us more," begged Nimida.

"They are confusing in many ways. They seem to appreciate comfort. Their sleeping mats are raised off the floor and are incredibly fluffy and pleasurable. But on the other hand, their clothing is torture. Their foot coverings pinch, and their waistbands are way too tight. I was glad to get out of them the first chance I had," Oh'Dar added.

"I would like to see you in them sometime, would you mind?" asked Tehya.

"I could do that. You definitely have an eye for different wrappings."

"Oh, you do not know, Oh'Dar," exclaimed Nimida. "We have been wearing the same old coverings all our lives, and Tehya now has us excited about new designs."

"I wish the males would consider wearing wrappings. I think they would look attractive in them," added Tehya.

"I can hear them now, 'Only females, the elderly, and the Waschini wear wrappings. Males do not wear wrappings!'" and Nadiwani impersonated a male's voice mocking the idea.

"But what of the Brothers? All the Brothers wear wrappings; if you've ever been to their village, you'll know that Chief Ogima Adoeete wears very decorative ones. And so does Oh'Dar. I see nothing wrong with it," pointed out Nootau.

"Why do you not start wearing them, Nootau? You could lead the way," Nimida said with a sparkle in her eyes.

"You are teasing me, but I just might. Wait and see."

"Oh'Dar, could you teach us how to make necklaces like the one Khon'Tor had you make for Tehya?" asked Nimida. 'And stitch on the beads? We cannot do such fine work as you can—though we want to try our hands at it."

Nootau spoke up, "I need to take Kweeuu out. Do you want to come with me?"

They all nodded and went on a walk down one of the paths leading away from Kthama to the spot prepared long ago for Kweeuu's use. They chatted and laughed as they walked, Oh'Dar keeping his eye on Tehya the whole way. Her wolf guard took up the rear, several paces behind.

From far above in the treetops surrounding Kthama's entrance, someone was watching. Someone with patience and a plan. Someone who had nothing but time on his hands to study the watchers' shifts. Someone who did not make it home to Kayerm before twilight that night.

CHAPTER 8

The group spent the day together, after which Oh'Dar found his parents at their usual mealtime table.

"Did you have a good first day back, son?" asked Acaraho.

"It was wonderful. I see Nimida and Nootau are very close, like brother and sister. And I am very happy that Tehya and Khon'Tor are going to have another offspring."

"Your mother and I wonder if perhaps you are ready for your own quarters here? Now that your Workshop has been forfeited to the females," said Acaraho.

"I would appreciate that. If there is room—"

"We already have several picked out for you to choose from. Do not worry, they are not on top of ours—so you will have your privacy," Acaraho smiled.

Privacy for what, thought Oh'Dar. *I will not be paired any time soon—the female I wanted is promised to another.*

"I stopped at the Brothers on the way here," he said, then paused. "Acise is promised to one of the braves. Did you know?" he asked.

Adia looked at Acaraho with a pained expression.

"No, we did not. I am sorry to hear that," she sighed. Acaraho took her hand under the table.

"It is my own fault. I do not know what to do."

"You said *promised*—" said Adia.

"That is what her mother said. Acise noticed me and then turned and walked away. I fear I have hurt her very much."

"I am not telling you to interfere, but from what you just said, she still has feelings for you. Only you can decide what to do next, son," said Acaraho.

"It is of no use. She has moved on. But I do not know how to. Now that I figured out what I want, it is too late."

They sat silently for a while, giving him space for his feelings to settle.

"I do want to spend some time there with Honovi and Is'Taqa, though. I also want to replenish the supplies for Tehya and her friends. And gather some stones from the rock beds along the river before it gets too cold. But I am not ready yet.

"And I do not want to think about who it is. Maybe Pajackok, or maybe Isskel? Both are good hunters, skilled riders, and expert tool makers. Both would provide well for her," he added, absent-mindedly.

Oh'Dar put his head down and laid it on his arms. Acaraho rested a hand on his son's back.

"I never told you what your name means, Oh'Dar," said Adia suddenly. "And why I picked that name for you."

Not looking up, Oh'Dar replied a muffled, "No, you said you would tell me someday when I was older."

"When I left Kthama on the morning I found you, I was on my way to take Goldenseal to Ithua. Nadiwani did not want me to go. Khon'Tor was away at a High Council meeting, so I was next in charge, and you know how much Nadiwani worries anyway. She offered to take the roots herself or to send someone else. And she was right, but I could not shake the feeling that I had to make the trip. Nadiwani finally agreed that she felt it too. Once I had decided I was going, a sense of calm came over me, and I knew that it was what the Mother wanted. Though I did not know why."

She paused.

"And you know the rest of the story of how I found you and brought you back. When Nadiwani and I were checking you over, we realized you needed a name. I suggested Oh'Dar."

"So, you made up a name for me?" he raised his head to ask.

"That is what everyone thinks. But let me tell you the rest of the story," she continued.

"You know that my mother died giving birth to me. But just before I was born, she told my father about a dream she had the night before. She was in a beautiful forest, and the sky overhead was a deep blue. So deep a blue that it was unnatural, and it struck her so. As she was standing there, dark clouds formed, and the wind picked up. Before long, the storm became so strong that she was frightened. The darker the skies became, the more her fear grew. She found a small alcove to hide in, and just as she thought the storm would overtake her, the skies cleared, and a bird with the brightest blue feathers she had ever seen came and landed before her. He had a beautiful stone in his mouth that he laid at her feet. As she bent to pick it up, the bird spoke. He said that he was sent by the Great Spirit to tell her that the daughter she was carrying would become a great blessing to the People. And that through this daughter would come another great blessing. And she should name him Oh'Dar. And then the bird flew away and my mother woke up with a great feeling of peace and calm. The next morning, she died, giving me life."

Oh'Dar had looked up to listen to the story. The tears in his mother's eyes told him this was very sacred to her and hard to share.

"I have never talked about my mother's dream with anyone but my father. I do not know what your path is, Oh'Dar. But I know that you are here for a reason, and whatever it is, it will be enough," she said.

"What was the stone the bird brought, Mama?" he asked.

"It was a deep red jasper," she said.

"The same I picked for the necklace I made you," he exclaimed and sat up further.

"Yes, the same necklace I put around your neck when you last left so you would have to come back to me," she said.

Oh'Dar opened his shirt to show her that he was wearing it. He had not forgotten.

He reached up to pull it over his head and put it around his mother's neck. "You promised me that when I returned, you would start wearing it."

"When I saw it after you had left it for me, Oh'Dar, I knew then that you were on the path you needed to be and that I had to let you find your own way home."

Oh'Dar got up and came around to wrap his arms around her neck.

"I know this is where I belong now, Mother. And no matter if I have to go back to Shadow Ridge from time to time, I will never stay away forever," he said as he breathed deeply of her familiar scent.

Acaraho and Adia were pleased to see the smile return to their Waschini son's face.

"Do you want to see the rooms you may choose from for your very own?" asked Acaraho.

"I am ready," said Oh'Dar, and they got up and left toward the tunnel to the first level living quarters.

Adia and Acaraho had picked rooms on the first level as Oh'Dar did not have the same low-light vision as the People. They went through them all, with Oh'Dar picking the last. It had the most natural light and turned out to be the closest to what had been Acaraho's quarters, which he now shared with Adia.

Adia and Nadiwani still used the Healer's Quarters for their work area, and there were sleeping mats in case of an emergency, but the space had become more of a healing facility now that nobody lived there permanently.

Adia could tell that Oh'Dar was pleased with the quarters he had chosen. "You may want to ask your friends to help you fix it up. I am sure they would be glad to, and I am sure they will not mind if you take your bed and any other personal items out of the workshop."

I must remember to make a new hiding place for Ben's pistol in the new quarters, Oh'Dar thought.

"That is a great idea, Mama. I will do that, and I will ask the others for their help." He hugged them both.

Now that Oh'Dar was back, Khon'Tor decided it was time to bring his inner circle together again.

The Leader came in with Tehya, Third Rank, to find the others already seated. Acaraho, the High Protector, Adia, the Healer and Second Rank, Nadiwani, the Healer's Helper, First Guard Awan, Mapiya, who represented the females, Urilla Wuti, and now Oh'Dar were all present. Khon'Tor was not yet sure about Oh'Dar's role, only that it seemed he somehow completed the circle.

"Thank you for coming," he started as he watched Tehya take her seat next to Urilla Wuti with Kweeuu close behind. "I am, as we all are, pleased that Oh'Dar has come home. I have also asked Urilla Wuti to join our circle while she is with us. As I was walking here, I realized that you are, each in your own way, someone I trust and on whom I depend. Beyond the ranks set in the second laws, you have become my own Circle of Council of sorts. So that is what I will now refer to you as.

"We have received word that, despite our great care and our belief that it had run its course, the sickness was taken back after the High Council meeting and is spreading through the other communities. We do not know the effects yet.

"Perhaps we were lucky not to lose more than we did, but we have no idea yet how many of our males might be sterile. Only time will tell us that. All of you in this room were here when Haan came to the High Council meeting and told us the stories of the

Fathers—the Mothoc. Adia and Acaraho, have you told Oh'Dar what has happened since he left Kthama?"

"Yes," answered Acaraho.

"About Akar, too?"

"Yes."

"Very well, so we are now waiting for Haan to return to open Kthama Minor. Lifrin died with whatever secrets were supposed to be passed on to Adia. When Haan came to collect Akar, he told us that our Healers needed to prepare for the opening of Kthama Minor. He mentioned a ritual but had no knowledge of what it was. Haan is treating this as a very serious matter, so we must, too. We are dealing with mysteries here, the nature and power of which we have no inkling. It may only be superstition, but we cannot take the chance that it is not."

Oh'Dar asked, "No one but the Healers of the High Rocks had this information?"

"That is what Haan said. It was passed down through the generations but only through the Healers here," Khon'Tor answered. "I imagine that is because this was the birthplace of the Wrak-Wavara —it started *and ended* here.

The room was silent, the atmosphere thick with concern.

"Perhaps we should send the Healers away until after this is over. We cannot risk anything happening to them, and we do not know what we are dealing with," said Acaraho, worry lining his brow.

"But what if we serve a role? What if we have to be here for some reason, and they cannot open Kthama Minor without us?" asked Adia.

"If you serve a role you do not understand and are harmed by not being prepared, then what is the gain? No. Unless we get some answers, some *real* answers, I forbid it," said Acaraho.

Adia raised her eyebrows.

"I do not know that you have the authority to do that," she replied.

Acaraho stood up. "Perhaps not as the High Protector, but I am your mate, Adia. And I will not risk you any more than Khon'Tor would risk Tehya."

"Acaraho is right, Adia. We will not risk you, or Nadiwani or Urilla Wuti. We have to find another way," said Khon'Tor.

"If you try to save the few of us, you might lose the chance to save all the People. I do not think it is a fair trade," said Adia.

Acaraho was at the end of his nerves. "I said no."

Adia's eyes flared at her mate. "You are being self-ish," she said.

"Selfish? Well, if I am, I do not care. I have a right to be, for once. No one has been more dedicated to our people than I, but I will not risk what I have waited my entire life for and feared I would never have."

"But what about the first law, that the needs of the community—"

"*Quat! Rok* the first laws," Acaraho spat out, and

his arm sliced through the air. "*What good are rules and laws if they cost us that which makes our very life worth living*?"

Everyone looked at each other, never having heard Acaraho talk this way, or use such language, let alone in front of females.

Oh'Dar slapped his hands on his knees and also stood up. He paced as he spoke. "Well, if no one else has the answers, and there is no way to find out what this preparation ritual is, then the solution is simple. All we have to do is go back in time and ask Lifrin herself," Oh'Dar added, trying to break the tension.

Urilla Wuti and Adia stopped, looked at each other, and then looked at Khon'Tor.

"What? What are you thinking?" the Leader asked.

Silence.

"*What*?"

"Give us a few days to investigate," said Urilla Wuti.

Khon'Tor frowned at the older Healer but remembered that Adia had told him Urilla Wuti had special abilities. He assumed it had something to do with those.

"Alright. I know this is a difficult time. I think we all need a break from this unrelenting tension. Especially Acaraho. You are correct, Acaraho. No one, including me, has given more in service to the People of the High Rocks. And no one is going to do anything to put Adia, or anyone else, in harm's way."

Acaraho held up a hand and turned away, gathering his self-control.

"On a happier note, Tehya is due in a few weeks," said Adia, staring at the back of her mate.

The others smiled, and the tension relaxed somewhat.

"And Oh'Dar has a place of his own now. Nootau, Nimida, and some of his other friends are helping him fix it up," she added.

"Does that mean you have found your place, Oh'Dar?" asked Khon'Tor.

"Yes, Khon'Tor. I have. Here, as one of the People. As it should be," he replied.

Adia's eyes lit up, but she did not comment.

Awan spoke, "Do you still wish to keep the guards around your quarters, Khon'Tor?"

"Yes, for the time being. Even though Akar is gone, I doubt his bad feelings toward me have."

"Anything else?"

Oh'Dar spoke up, looking over at Kweeuu curled up around Tehya's feet.

"Yes, Khon'Tor. You owe me a wolf. Your mate seems to have stolen mine."

Everyone laughed, as Kweeuu never seemed to leave Tehya's side, even with Oh'Dar's return.

After Khon'Tor had dismissed his Circle, Acaraho stopped Adia and Urilla Wuti some way down the corridor. "What are you planning to do?"

"Let us go to the Healer's Quarters, and we will explain. But not out here in the open," Adia answered.

Sensing Acaraho's ongoing agitation, Nadiwani followed Tehya, leaving the three of them to make their way to the Healer's Quarters.

By the time they got there, Acaraho's patience had expired.

"Alright. Now explain what is going on. I know you have something in mind because I saw the look that passed between you when Oh'Dar joked about going back in time. Surely that is not possible."

"I cannot say whether it is possible or not; I can only say that I do not know how to do it," answered Urilla Wuti.

"*Va!*" Acaraho slammed his fist down on the work table. "By the Great Spirit, never a straight answer. Just promise me that whatever you are going to do is not dangerous."

Adia had seen Acaraho lose his temper only a handful of times, the first being when she told him that she had been seeded by Khon'Tor's attack. But she did not remember him using such language.

She went over and put her hand on his arm. He jerked it away and covered his face with his hands.

"I cannot lose you, Adia. I waited for this all my life, never thinking it would happen. I do not care what secrets Kthama Minor holds. There is nothing worth risking your life over."

"I promise you that what we are about to do is not dangerous. And if it works, it will give us the answers we need to make the preparations Haan says must be done," she said, looking deeply into his eyes. "I would never do anything to risk leaving you. Never."

Acaraho pulled his hands away from his face.

"I am sorry. Sometimes I forget how much pressure you are under," she said.

Acaraho took her in his arms and held her for some time. Urilla Wuti waited patiently, happy to see them so bonded and in love.

Finally, Acaraho released his mate.

"Then I will let you get to what you need to do. I will be off duty early tonight, and I am going to eat in our quarters if you wish to join me."

Adia nodded and leaned up to give him a hug. She watched him leave, his body tense and tight. *I have neglected him,* she admonished herself.

Then she turned back to Urilla Wuti. "Do you think it will work?"

"All we can do is try. When will you be ready?" Urilla Wuti asked.

"I am ready now if you are. I will tell the guards outside to let no one enter, so we are not disturbed."

I do not need the guards any longer; I should tell Acaraho. Hakani is gone, and there is no longer any threat, so I am sure they can be put to better use elsewhere.

The two Healers took their places on the sleeping mats at the back of the room. They would be entering the Corridor. Once there, they would lose connection with their bodies, so the safest position was lying prone in a protected environment.

Adia felt the familiar portal opening, and within moments, she was standing in the same beautiful setting as before—the clearing under a canopy of trees. The sky was the same vibrant blue, and encircling the perimeter were wildflowers made up of textures and colors she could not begin to describe. In the distance were the high rocks of Kthama. And there, again, was the Presence, the comforting abiding *something* that was always there, permeating everything with its rich, sweet, gentle vibration.

As she adjusted to being in this place again, Adia saw that Urilla Wuti was by her side. This time the other Healer was as she appeared in their world now. She had not assumed the form of her younger, vibrant self as she had the previous time.

Without need for words, the two stood silently, giving gratitude for the divine benevolence that could create such a place of peace and beauty for its offspring. The air was crystal clear and had a freshness that filled Adia's lungs with joy as she inhaled. Every movement felt almost musical—as if she were one with all of creation, and that all separation was just an illusion. For the first time since she had first come here, she noticed the feel of sunlight on her skin, and its warmth swept over her like liquid. Everywhere was pleasure and delight and joy.

Adia could not tell whether time was passing, only that the desire to stay was becoming stronger and stronger. Then, she felt herself pulled back into her body in the Healer's Quarters.

Adia opened her eyes and turned to the older Healer. "Did you bring us back? What happened?"

"No, I did not bring you back. You know I do not have the power to override your will. I brought myself back. On some level below conscious thought, I realized that my desire to stay was starting to become too strong," she explained.

"You are right. I realized it too just before I returned. It did not work, Urilla Wuti. What do we do now?" Adia asked.

"We will keep trying. Neither of us has a tie to Lifrin, so it is not as easy. But we will not give up. Lifrin is our only hope."

"I am exhausted, even though nothing happened." Adia closed her eyes.

"We will try again tomorrow. Get some rest and then spend the evening with your mate. He needs you." And Urilla Wuti got up to go to her own quarters.

Adia wanted nothing more than to close her eyes, but instead, she rose to go. *Urilla Wuti is right; I am too busy being the People's Healer. I forget that even the strongest of us also need comfort, help, support.*

Acaraho practically dragged himself back to his quarters. He had meant to bring some food from the eating area, but he was too tired to go back and too worried to care. He entered and immediately smelled lavender, and what he thought might be geranium. Their quarters were lit with a soft glow. Adia was sitting there waiting for him, an array of small containers next to their sleeping mat.

She held out her hand for him to join her.

"What is this?" he asked.

"Come. Lie down. Let me tend to you. And afterward, I will bring you something refreshing to eat. I have it all prepared."

"I am sorry I was cross." He took her hand and sat down next to her.

"I forget how much responsibility you carry. It is I who must apologize. But I promise you, again, nothing Urilla Wuti and I are doing is dangerous. It is the opposite; it is what we need to do to be as safe as possible."

He raised her hand and pressed it to his lips. Then, looking around, he asked, "What do you want me to do?"

"Just stretch out and relax and let me minister to you. Nothing is required but to enjoy the moment. If you fall asleep, we will eat when you awake."

Acaraho did as she instructed and spent the next few hours enjoying her loving touch. The oils spread smoothly under the warmth of her hand as she kneaded the tightness out of his muscles. She was passing her hands over his chest, his arms, his thighs, and he could not help but let out moans of pleasure. "Will I not need to wash these off afterward?" he asked sleepily.

"Sssh, yes, but that is all taken care of. Khon'Tor has given permission for me to light a fire to warm the water, and I will clean all of this off of you after we are finished."

"It feels wonderful. Thank you, Saraste'."

Adia leaned forward and kissed him. "Roll over," she said sweetly and returned to where his body was holding most of his tension. It was hard work, but a pleasure at the same time, as she passed her hands across his steely back, down over his hips, feeling the tightness in his thighs yield under her pressure, admiring his physique in the dim light as she worked. She had forgotten for a while how magnificent he was, and she pushed her rising ardor away, wanting to focus on relieving the muscular tension. As she wove her fingers in between his toes, she heard him chuckle, and it made her smile.

When she had finished, Adia went to get the warm water. She set the first bowl down next to the mat. Taking the scraps of woven cloths she had prepared, she dipped them in the soapy water and began cleaning off the oils with which she had just covered him, head to toe. The sounds of pleasure he made melted her heart, and she was ashamed at how she had let other matters take first place. She then returned the first bowl to the flames and brought the second for a rinse.

"Roll over once more, my love," she said, then finished cleaning the oils off his front. She was happy to see him surrender to sleep just as she was about done. After completing both rounds, she extinguished the flame and returned to the mat. Tired herself, she covered him up with the heavy pelt and lay down next to him, thanking the Great Mother for giving her such a male to love and with whom to share her life.

Within a few hours, she awoke to find Acaraho pressed up behind her. He slipped her long dark hair aside and began slowly kissing her neck. His lips were soft yet strong. She let her own little sounds of pleasure escape, and felt his body tense against her back. He snaked his arm around her waist, and more demanding, pulled her back against him. Knowing he wanted her made Adia's heart pound and she sighed and let the waves of pleasure cover her, enjoying the warmth of his lips and breath on her skin. After a moment, she turned to face him, welcoming his advances and raising a leg to rest it over his hips. He grabbed the crook of her leg and pulled her up against him, conveying his intent to take her.

"Always, forever, only you," she whispered. Then he claimed her, and they found their rhythm as only those can who have loved for a time together. Their bond with each other was sacred and profound, and she lost herself in the ecstasy of the physical expression of their mutually captured hearts and souls. Tears of happiness pricked her eyes when he finally found release, knowing that, this night, he would sleep soundly and escape his troubles, at least for a while.

The next day, Urilla Wuti and Adia re-entered the Corridor and again tried to contact Lifrin—with the same results.

As they were puzzling over their failure, Urilla Wuti said, "We have no previous relationship with Lifrin. We must find someone who knew her or something of hers that is still here—some physical way to contact her. Is there anyone here who is a relation?"

"Lifrin had a younger brother, Tar. We can talk to him, but we cannot tell him what we are doing. I do not even know how she died; it is not spoken of," added Adia.

Tar had no idea who the older female with the Healer was, but he did know Adia. They had not spoken much since she first came to Kthama. She had tried to talk with him, but Tar made it clear he did not want anything to do with her, so Adia had respected his wishes and kept her distance. Since then, he had almost entirely kept to himself. Now, seeing Adia approach, he suddenly felt embarrassed by his previous actions. He put down what he was working on and rose to greet them.

"Greetings, Tar, this is Urilla Wuti—the Healer of the People of the Far High Hills. She is visiting with us for a while. I know we have not spoken much, and I am sorry for this to be our first real conversation, but we need to know something about your sister, Lifrin. I apologize if it is difficult for you."

Tar motioned for them to sit down. "What would you like to know about her? It has been a long time; I am not sure how far I will be able to help you. I was very young when she—" He paused.

"Is there, by any chance, something personal of hers that you own?"

Tar thought for a moment. Their parents had passed before Lifrin did, and she had raised him on her own for the few years she still lived. After she died, he had stayed in their family quarters since the familiar surroundings were all he had left for comfort, though they were also painful. He had been assigned an older female to look in on him and take care of his needs. As Tar grew older, a male was appointed to make sure he learned a craft so he could function as part of the community.

"I cannot think of a single thing," he replied. He

remembered Lifrin's Keeping Stone, but he did not think they meant anything like that.

Urilla Wuti sighed. Without some tangible remnant of her life here, it might be impossible to contact her.

In the silence, Adia wondered what had happened to Lifrin. She wanted to ask but did not want to be insensitive.

"I could take you to where she was killed," he said quietly.

The two females were shocked but tried to hide it. Adia wondered if they were truly about to find out the great mystery surrounding the previous Healer's death.

"Is it far?" asked Urilla Wuti.

"It is down along the lowest level of Kthama. No one goes there. It was, well, you will see. Would that help you?"

"I am not sure, Tar. We do not want to upset you," added Adia.

"It was a long time ago. I still miss her every day, but I have learned to live with it. It is odd that you would come on the anniversary of her death."

Urilla Wuti and Adia looked at each other. It was Adia who spoke. "We had no idea, Tar. I am sorry; are you sure this is not too much for you?"

"It is alright. The hardest part, learning to live without her, is long past. If you have time, we can go now, but it will be a bit of a walk," he added.

Adia wondered if Urilla Wuti was up to this.

"I will be fine," answered the older Healer, picking up Adia's concern.

Tar put his tools away and then led them slowly and carefully through the winding tunnels of Kthama's lower levels.

Adia wondered if they would find their way back, should something happen to him; it seemed like they walked forever. Along the way, there were large pillars of stone and locust propped up along the sides of the tunnels, and she became a little uncomfortable. *I remember this. I came this way when I first arrived at Kthama and was learning the layout. Even before I saw the propped up supports, I had a terrible feeling about it. When I asked later, the First Guard warned me never to come this way again. If Acaraho knew I was down here, oh my—*

"Is it much farther?" she asked, having now passed the point where, long ago, she had turned back.

"No. We are as far as we can go," and Tar stopped.

"Up ahead, do you see that huge collection of tumbled rock that blocks the way?"

Adia peered through the dark and saw it, as did Urilla Wuti.

"Yes."

"That is where she died. They never got her body out. It is buried under the rock, back there some distance," he said quietly. "There was no way to do it without risking more lives," he added.

Adia put her hand on his arm, to comfort him,

the horror of the circumstances of Lifrin's death just sinking in. *She died in a rock slide. And they could not get her out to give her a decent burial. How terrible. I can understand that it was too dangerous to try.*

Standing there, both Urilla Wuti and Adia could get a sense of Lifrin and who she was. "Your sister was a very giving person, was she not?" said Urilla Wuti.

"She was the best. She had an amazing heart. Even though I was young when she passed, I still remember her. She would do anything for anyone. She sacrificed her life for his," he added.

Adia looked confused, as Tar was speaking as if they knew the story.

"For whose, Tar?"

"For Khon'Tor, the Leader. I thought you knew that," he said. "For both of them."

"No, we did not."

"They were down here trying to shore up a weakened section of this tunnel. Another male had been injured by falling rock. Lifrin was here trying to relieve his pain—I was told it was obvious he was not going to make it and that they had no hope of freeing him. Khon'Tor and the High Protector were here with them, holding up the posts they had used to support the collapsing tunnel. In this kind of dangerous job, Khon'Tor would help alongside the High Protector, as they were the largest and strongest males. Just before it happened, Lifrin must have had a premonition that the tunnel roof was going to collapse because she warned them in time. The roof came down on her, and the male she was trying to help. The male would not have made it either way, but she definitely saved the lives of both Khon'Tor and the High Protector."

Both the Healers could have cried. What a heart-breaking story.

Adia wondered if Tar blamed Khon'Tor and Acaraho but did not want to ask that, either.

"After that, the Leader and the High Protector never worked together on dangerous projects again. It was too close a call; they were almost both killed."

For a minute, no one spoke, and then Tar continued, "Khon'Tor, he can be so fierce, or at least he used to be. He seems to have changed the past year or so. But he checked on me often that first year after Lifrin was killed. The High Protector made arrangements for one of the females to take care of me. And later, a male mentor. I think he would have taken me under his wing himself, except that every time I looked at him, I practically broke down, remembering her death. I finally grew up, got on my feet, and told him that I no longer needed the help he was providing. But I will not forget that kindness.

I never blamed them; that was just the way Lifrin was. She gave her life for theirs."

Urilla Wuti and Adia were silent.

After a moment, Urilla Wuti spoke, "I am sorry, Tar. I cannot imagine your anguish. It is to your credit that you never blamed Khon'Tor or the High

Protector. That speaks highly of you, and the values Lifrin instilled. I am sure you miss her very much."

"I do. But as I said, I have learned to live with it. I wish I had paired, but I know I am afraid of suffering another loss like that. It is not worth the risk," he replied, unguarded for a moment.

"Thank you for bringing us here, Tar. I am sure this was hard for you. I wish I had not had to take you up on your offer," Adia apologized.

"I would have visited here anyway. I have come every year on this day from the time I was old enough. I am sure I am not supposed to be down here, but I still come. It is the last place she was; it makes me feel close to her to be here."

Tar leaned down and picked up a small rock and handed it to Adia. "This is as good as anything personal."

She took it from him quietly, reverently.

They walked back in silence. The Healers thanked Tar again and left him to his grieving, slowly making their way back to the Healer's Quarters.

Once back, they sat down, and Adia placed the rock in front of them. "I had no idea," she said.

"Such sorrow. Such a terrible loss. No wonder it is not spoken of; it would be irreverent to make it part of idle conversation," said Urilla Wuti.

"Acaraho has never mentioned it to me. I have so

many questions. Why could she not save herself? Was there no time for them to get her out too? But I did not want to pry. Do you think this will help us connect with her?"

"It is as good a chance as we are going to get. It saddens me to think of that as her final place—that she never had a proper farewell." Urilla Wuti sat for a moment. "Shall we try again?"

Adia nodded, reverently picking up the rock, and the two females went over to the mats where they could relax and leave their bodies safe. Adia gently placed the rock between them, and they each put a hand on it. Both created an intention to contact Lifrin, and Urilla Wuti opened the portal.

Within moments, they were back in the Corridor, in the same beautiful clearing as before. Once again, Adia marveled at the beauty, the peace, the Presence she always encountered there. Almost no time had passed when they saw a figure coming toward them. It was a female, but never having met Lifrin, they had no idea if it could be her. They had forgotten to ask for a description, though she could have appeared any way she wished.

Somehow they understood it *was* her. She smiled at them kindly, a tall, graceful figure wearing a flowing full-length wrapping of sparkling purple. The grass seemed to give way under her feet, turning iridescent in the depression of her steps.

"Greetings, Adia, Healer of the High Rocks, and Urilla Wuti, Healer of the Far High Hills," she said—

though Adia was never sure if she heard words or if they just appeared in her mind. She was not even going to ask how Lifrin knew who they were; Urilla Wuti had taught her to suspend critical thinking in this place because its workings could not be understood from what they knew of their own realm.

"We are pleased you came to greet us. Thank you," said Urilla Wuti.

"You have just come from speaking with Tar. My brother still grieves, I know. I look forward to when we are reunited. I wish I could tell him that I am happy—that I still live. I wish he would grasp hold of life instead of letting it pass by him as he is doing," said Lifrin quietly. "But we each have our own path.

"You have questions, no doubt. Let me try to answer them," she continued. Her voice had an almost lyrical quality about it. "You want to know what I should have passed on to you, Adia, about Kthama Minor. It is only your work with Urilla Wuti that makes it possible for us to do this.

"I know that the Sarnonn, Haan, has made contact and that they are about to open Kthama Minor. The Sarnonn Leader has told you correctly; you need to prepare before the seal is broken, and it is imperative that you do. If you do not, there is a chance that you will not survive it."

Adia let out a sigh of relief that they had found a way to contact Lifrin.

"But before I continue with that, you have questions about why I did not try to save myself in the tunnel collapse—was there not time? It is important that you understand so you can make peace with my sacrifice. I was attending to one of the males who had gotten badly hurt in a collapse farther down from where your Leader Khon'Tor and the High Protector were helping. I was called there to give him something for pain, for it was obvious that he would not survive his injuries. As I was tending to him, I had a very clear vision of what was to come. Your mate and Khon'Tor were holding up the crumbling roof. It was a tremendous weight, and I could tell they were weakening. And at that moment, I knew that it was my time to move on—that I was not meant to survive. But I also knew that it was just as imperative that Khon'Tor and Acaraho *did* survive."

Adia asked anyway, "Can you tell us why? Or is it not for us to know?"

"It is crucial that you know. It is another reason that our connecting is important—so you will understand more of how everything works to the good, and that my death was not the tragedy it appears. I had to leave, Healer, to make way for you to come."

Lifrin's words hit Adia like a physical blow.

"Yes, there was time for one of them to save me, but I also saw at that moment that if I did, one of them would not survive. And it was important that they both lived, just as it was important that I did not."

Lifrin looked off in the distance, tears welling in her eyes.

"My only regret is leaving my brother alone."

Adia was surprised that there could be sorrow here. It confused her, and she would have to ask Urilla Wuti later.

Lifrin collected herself and continued, "As far as Kthama Minor is concerned, I will only tell you what I would have told you in the other lifetime. The secret of Kthama Minor has for generations been kept by the Healer of the People of the High Rocks. Even the story of Wrak-Wavara, the Age of Darkness —when the Ancients betrayed the trust between our people and the Brothers—is known only to a few. It is a dark stain on our past.

"Kthama Minor is a separate system of caves, and it was a central place of operation during the Age of Darkness. Then it was sealed by the Ancients, and from that point on, very little was ever spoken of its existence. Before they left, the Ancients initiated a Rah'hora, the terms of which were that we were never to speak openly of the Wrak-Wavara.

"These are the words they left with the People. *We are Mothoc. We are keepers of the Others. What had to be done was done. But no more. Never again, the Wrak-Wavara. The Others who are our wards are now your Brothers. Learn their language, make amends, regain their trust. Leader to next Leader—Kthama Healer to next Kthama Healer—only these may speak of this past. This is Rah-hora. We leave you to the future of your own making. When the Wrak-Ayya falls, the Age of Shadows, the true test will begin. We will be watching.*"

. . .

A chill passed through both Adia and Urilla Wuti simultaneously.

"As you speak it, Healer Lifrin, the People have not violated the Rah'hora," Adia whispered. "But Haan made it sound as if it had been broken," she added.

"Perhaps theirs was different. Perhaps they were given different terms," said Urilla Wuti.

"I remember Haan saying that they were to have no contact with us. Yet our instructions were to make amends to the Brothers, with a prohibition against speaking openly of Wrak-Wavara," Adia said. "And yet, Haan told us there was a threat in their Rah'hora —that if they contacted us, we would all be destroyed. It does not make sense."

"Perhaps in time, it will," said Urilla Wuti, tempted to ask about this but already knowing Lifrin would not speak of it. "Healer, you have information for us about preparation?"

Lifrin answered. "I do not know how far the Ancients could see or what they could see, but they must have known that at some point the Sassen would open Kthama Minor because they told Kthama's Healer how to prepare for it when the time came. The information was given only to her and passed on from Healer to Healer until my death broke the chain.

"The Ancients had abilities of which only a

shadow remains in the People, and then mostly with those who are recognized as Healers. Our seventh sense is a pale echo of their abilities. When they closed Kthama Minor, they covered it with energy, so we could not sense its true past. When the Sassen break the seal, all that blocked energy will be released. For those who have a heightened seventh sense, that can be deadly.

"If you do not prepare, the wave of energy that will be unleashed has the power to overwhelm you. You have both made Connections; you understand that we cannot make them with new or very young offspring because they cannot assimilate adult experiences. The energy of pain and suffering, self-doubt, grief, fear, would destroy them because they have not been prepared by life to bear those feelings. They are not well enough prepared to go through what we went through as part of our paths. And it is our paths that prepare us for our paths—if that makes sense."

Lifrin continued, "When Kthama Minor is uncovered, it will be difficult enough for everyone—most likely everyone present will feel it to one extent or another. But when the inner seals are broken, the level will change entirely. It is this for which you must prepare, for the same reason that offspring cannot handle adult experiences, you will be bombarded by all the stored-up energy within Kthama Minor being released at once. And especially you, Adia, because of your condition."

"My *condition*?"

"You are seeded, Adia. I am allowed to tell you this because Kthama Minor will be opened before you can realize it. You must take care of yourself for your own sake and that of the soul destined to come through you."

Adia staggered. *I am seeded with Acaraho's offspring; Great Mother, thank you.* "But what if we had not found you? I would not have known. Would the Great Mother have allowed my offspring to be damaged if we had not discovered a way to contact you?"

"It was ordained that you contact me in time, Adia. Just as it was part of the great plan, the Order of Functions, that I chose to leave and save the Leader and the High Protector. Just as it was destined for you to find and rescue Oh'Dar. Perhaps this will help build your faith in the love and good intentions of the One-Who-Is-Three."

Adia's head was spinning. *What was pre-destined, and what was free will? If it was destined for Lifrin to die, then did she* not *have free will in choosing whether to save them or herself? Did the One know what she would choose before she chose it? Or did she only have belief in free will?* And if Lifrin had not chosen as she did, what would Adia's life have been like? Never to come to Kthama, never to rescue Oh'Dar, never to have the love she shared with Acaraho? With effort, she brought herself back to the moment.

"How do we prepare, Lifrin?" asked Urilla Wuti,

"And if this is only for Kthama's Healers, why am I here?"

Adia was surprised that Urilla Wuti had questions, only now realizing she had unconsciously thought her mentor knew everything. *She is also still learning.*

"What is ordered for one time is not necessarily ordered for another. You are here because you are supposed to be." Lifrin said it with no judgment or criticism.

Urilla Wuti nodded, realizing that Lifrin was wary of saying too much and affecting her path.

"Normally, when we as Healers prepare, we focus on opening—on increasing our sensitivity to guidance, impressions, visions. In this case, you must do the opposite. You must armor and steel yourself against these influences. You must strengthen your boundaries. The work you have done in controlling the depth of the Connections you establish will help you achieve this. You are already working on restricting the flow of information through your seventh senses."

"Could we not just leave Kthama? Go to one of the other Communities?" asked Adia, still processing that she was with offspring, and excited to tell Acaraho.

"You are tied to Kthama on planes other than the physical. Putting geographic distance between you and Kthama will have no effect."

I should have known that.

"Also, you need to be there. You both have critical roles to play in what will happen next—for the People and the Sarnonn."

Adia and Urilla Wuti exchanged a glance, only now realizing how intertwined they were in each other's lives.

"So how do we prepare, Healer?" asked Adia. They were ready to focus on this information now.

"As I said, you must shield your abilities; create energetic walls. To do this, you will need specific herbs and some meditative practices. You will also need to change your diets, though it will not hurt your offspring, Adia, I assure you of that."

The instructions were suddenly there in each female's mind.

"This is the opposite of everything we ordinarily do," said Urilla Wuti.

"Exactly," Lifrin nodded.

"How soon should we start?" questioned Adia.

"You have time. You can wait to begin until the moon is new, but no longer," Lifrin said.

Urilla Wuti and Adia both sensed that what needed to be achieved had taken place, and it was time to go. Neither of them had been in the Corridor this long before.

"Yes, it is time to part. I do not know if we will meet again. That is not shown to me. But if we need to, we will. I know you cannot give my love to Tar; oh, how I wish you could. But I will be grateful if you would encourage him to find a mate—if you do not object," Lifrin said in closing.

"We will do that, Lifrin. It is clear that he is lonely and on some level, even after so many years, still suffering," said Urilla Wuti.

With that, Lifrin turned and began to walk away as the others focused on creating the intention to return to their world. Within moments, they found themselves back on the sleeping mats in the Healer's Quarters.

Instinctively, neither female said anything, but each reached out to take the other's hand. They lay there for some time before Urilla Wuti went silently back to her quarters to process the experience in private. They knew that when their minds were clear, they would again meet together to discuss what had happened.

Adia curled into a fetal position. *I am seeded. I am going to have Acaraho's offspring.* She pondered awhile. *It is hard to understand how it all works. Lifrin giving her life, the information initially not passed down to me as it would have been—but now it is. Oh! But wait. If she had not died, I would not be here for her to give it. She said she had to leave so I could come. Was it destined for me to pair with Acaraho, just as I needed to be here to rescue Oh'Dar? It is too much to comprehend.*

And then the words of Urilla Wuti and her father came back to her— "*These are not things that worldly minds can understand.*" For the first time, she fully understood the meaning of the word faith.

CHAPTER 9

Hakani tossed and turned as she waited in their room for Akar'Tor to come home. Twilight had long passed, and it was well into the dark hours of the night. The next day came, and there was still no Akar'Tor.

That evening, she spoke to Haan. "Akar did not come home last night. And now it is well past twilight, but he still has not returned. I told you he was staying away all day, but at least then he was returning at nightfall. Do you not have any idea what he has been up to?"

"I do not. I have been occupied with the challenges of Tarnor and Dorn. I do not know that we have enough on our side to help the Akassa. I fear I will need to address the community again, though I do not wish to stir up more dissent. Tarnor is already doing his best to create hard feelings toward us. Perhaps I should focus instead on finding another place for us to live. It is becoming apparent that we cannot stay here."

"What do you mean? I thought you said that those who did not agree should leave Kayerm?"

"I did. But our numbers are far fewer than theirs. And if they leave, where will they go, except to take their anger elsewhere? And the most likely target would be the Akassa. If we remove ourselves as being the irritant, they will be able to continue their lives here. And hopefully, in time, their anger will dissipate."

"Winter is upon us. Do you have any idea where we will go?" she asked. "All the food stores are here at Kayerm."

Haan sighed. "The only place I can think of is Kthama."

Hakani's heart stopped. "Do you think that is possible, Haan? I mean, with how things are between Khon'Tor and Akar?" she did not add herself but, in her guilt, knew she should have. *I am so tired of all this turmoil in my head; how I wish it would end.*

"Right now, between all the males and females, there are thirty-nine of us, not counting you, Kalli, and Akar. If Akar were not in the picture, perhaps we could go to the Akassa, but the immense conflict between him and Khon'Tor changes that. And we cannot abandon our son." Haan sighed and sat down next to his mate and their daughter, who was nursing quietly.

"In ancient days, our people scoured the area to

find Kayerm. If there had been another suitable cave system nearby, I believe they would have found it. We know only of Kayerm and Kthama."

Silence.

Haan continued, "We cannot mix with them. We frighten them; I have seen it in their eyes and their reactions. They cannot help it, it is natural, and I did not help things when I lost control and almost killed Khon'Tor and the others when he was threatening you. I was at my limits with worry over you and Akar, but that does not change the damage I did."

"Khon'Tor would not want me back at Kthama, Haan. And that is aside from how he feels about Akar. I have done my part to damage our chances of that being an option. When you were at the High Council, was there no mention of any other Sassen?"

"No. All the People's communities sent sentries out to look, but, regardless, they would not be able to find any Sassen. The prohibition of contact is very strong. Between our natural ability to hide, and our cloaking fields, the Akassa would never find us unless we were willing that they should."

"What are you talking about, cloaking fields?"

"We have the ability to hide in what is essentially plain sight. We can extend the visual field of any background, so they do not see us. They simply over-look us, for lack of a better explanation."

"I have never heard you talk of this."

"There was no need. As long as we do not move, someone could be looking right at us and not see anything untoward. It is a holdover from the Moth-oc's abilities. Theirs were much more powerful even than that, which is why the Others seldom saw them. The Others were their wards, entrusted to them for help and protection, unaware of how much the Mothoc worked without their knowledge to help them. That is another reason the Wrak-Wavara was such a dark period— at the most intimate level, the Fathers-Of-Us-All betrayed those they were charged with watching over. Without Their Consent."

Hakani sat for a moment, mulling over what Haan was saying. "None of this is known to us. Perhaps to the High Council, but we were never told about this history. It is as if I do not even know who the People are anymore."

Uncharacteristically, she started to cry. "I cannot bear this any longer, Haan. Akar is gone, most of the others here are angry with us, and we do not even know where we are going to live. My head is playing tricks on me, and I am so confused. I should never have asked you to take us to Kthama. I should have died with Akar, and then none of this would have happened."

Haan lightly placed his huge hand on Hakani's back.

"It is just the current of life moving us forward. It was a miracle I found you floating on that log all those years ago. I do not know how you managed to cling to it as long as you did, but the fact that you did was because some part of you wanted to live; just as that same part had us reach out to the Akassa Healer for help. What is done is done. Somehow, I will find a place for us to go. Just try to stay focused on the troubles of the day and not think of the future. As for Akar, as I said before, he is a grown male, and whatever he is up to, there is nothing we can do to stop it. I only pray that for his sake, it has nothing to do with Kthama or Khon'Tor."

It was a long time since Hakani had let herself take any physical comfort from Haan, not wanting to instigate another mating session. Though he had said he would not expect that of her again, she did not want to take any chances. But she was so distraught that this once she leaned into him and let his huge body and warm hair-covering blanket her with a sense of protection.

Haan sighed. *She is truly troubled. One moment Hakani has glimpses of clarity about the part she plays in creating her own problems, and the next, she swings the other way and is overcome with hatred, jealousy, and accusation.*

Oh'Dar spent his days telling his mother and Nadi-wani about his studies and the different approach to medicine that the Waschini took. He explained how they were more dependent on reactive procedures than preventative measures, even cutting out areas of the body that they determined were diseased. His stories horrified them for the most part, though they tried to listen with open minds.

"Do you feel there is merit, Oh'Dar, in these approaches?"

"In some cases, yes. If the part of the body has putrefied, the blood supply cut off, then yes. But in my heart, I believe that our focus on maintaining health is a more effective approach than trying to address disease. I believe maintaining balance is the best course of action," he said.

Adia thought about this, "It is easy to get out of balance. I know Acaraho does not get enough sleep. And there are days that we do not get outside."

"Probably the only one who gets outside regularly is Kweeuu!" he joked.

"Well, there you go, we should all have turns taking him," Nadiwani laughed. "But good luck with that; the only one he seems to want to go anywhere with any more is Tehya," she added.

"Yes, I have lost my best friend. But it could not have been to a sweeter person," Oh'Dar added. He did not tell them that the last command he had given Kweeuu before leaving was to protect Tehya, though he believed that the wolf was also genuinely fond of her.

At the evening meal, Adia brought up Oh'Dar's observation that nearly everyone had become too busy to take a break and enjoy the outdoors, and how the tyranny of the immediate was taking first place in their lives.

"I should get out more, I know it," said Tehya. "Soon, I will be busy with our offspring. The only time I do get out is with Kweeuu, as you said, Oh'Dar."

"You need to let someone else take Kweeuu, Tehya. You are getting very close to delivery, and the thought of you out there going up and down the paths around Kthama worries me a little," said Adia.

"But my ever-present guard is always with me. So I am not out there alone. And I have my warmer wrappings now. But I understand what you are saying, and if you are worried, I am sure my mate would be even more so." She paused. "Tonight will be my last time, then, I promise. From now on, someone else is going to have to take him, but good luck luring him away," she chuckled.

Oh'Dar gave her a half frown, teasing her again about stealing his wolf.

They finished eating, and then Tehya got up, "I will be right back. Come on, Kweeuu," she said.

She and her guard left to take Kweeuu on his last walk with his beloved Tehya.

The others at the table watched her leave. "She is still carrying small," said Nadiwani.

"Yes, the offling is going to be small. But I am still not worried. I am glad it is a female; if it were a male, he would definitely be on the spindly side."

They laughed good-naturedly.

"Well, good! Then I would not be the only pitiful male at Kthama," Oh'Dar joked.

"Oh, you were so tiny, Oh'Dar. And so fragile. I was afraid to hold you at first. And you would turn pink, *pink,* when you cried. It took me a while to get used to it. But you have turned into a handsome male. I am sure the Waschini females noticed you, did they not?"

Oh'Dar almost blushed, and he lowered his head.

"It is true then," exclaimed Nimida. "So, was there no female you are interested in at this, what do you call it, Shadow Ridge?"

"No. I did have a teacher at one point that I favored. But it was just a crush."

"*Crush*?" asked Nimida, turning to the other females.

"It is a Waschini word, meaning something like infatuation. Passing fancy."

"*Passing fancy. Crush.* These are interesting terms," laughed Adia.

Nadiwani, not knowing any better, said, "Well, what about Acise, Oh'Dar? It seems like you two had some feelings for each other last time you were here."

Pain immediately crossed Oh'Dar's face. "Yes, I suppose that is true. I did stop at the Brothers on the way here, but Acise is promised to one of the braves."

"Oh. I am sorry," said Nadiwani.

"So am I," he said, looking away across the Great Chamber, trying to hide his emotions.

Nadiwani looked at Adia with apology written all over her face. She wanted to say something comforting but could not think of anything. She and Adia had both worried about who Oh'Dar would pair with once he was grown. When he and Acise had become interested in each other, it was like an answered prayer.

"Do you know who it is?" she asked, against her better judgment and knowing she should drop the subject.

"No. I need to go and see Ithua and Is'Taqa, though. I expect I will find out then. I want to be happy for her. I do. And I am. But I am sadder for myself, I guess. I know that sounds pathetic," he said.

"You have always felt your emotions strongly, Oh'Dar. It is nothing to apologize for. When you were little, you would just laugh and laugh with glee each time you knocked over the stacking stones or pulled apart one of my special plants. One time I looked away, just for a moment, and you stuffed half a plant in your mouth. You were so pleased with yourself—looking up at me with your smiling blue eyes and green pieces of mint sticking out of that silly grin of yours—that I could not even be mad at you."

Oh'Dar was still postponing his visit to the Brothers, dreading seeing Acise again. The thought of her spending her life with someone else cut him to the core. He wanted to distribute the presents he had brought for the Chiefs, Ithua, Honovi, and the others, but he was not ready to face his pain head-on by seeing Acise in person again so soon.

"Perhaps I will go in a few days. I know that I need to face it so I can move on."

Nadiwani could tell that Adia's heart was breaking for her son; as his honorary aunt, she was also feeling it.

They sat in silence for a while, waiting for Oh'Dar to process his feelings and for Tehya to return with Kweeuu.

Tehya walked carefully down the path from Kthama with the wolf running happily ahead. She wondered why he did not disappear for long periods of time. Surely he had needs to meet. But so far, he had stayed by her side pretty much the entire time since Oh'Dar had left several months ago. She had long since moved Kweeuu's sleeping mat into the Leader's Quarters since he stayed with her every night.

Her ever-present guard was not far behind her; she had wondered for some time if Mistok was perhaps afraid of the large grey wolf who had become her constant companion.

Kweeuu disappeared into the darkness farther down the trail. She thought she heard him growl, so she stopped to catch her breath and listen, and to let the guard catch up.

Suddenly, they both heard someone approaching from behind them. They turned, and Tehya heard the guard say, "Good evening, Adik'Tar, I did not hear you—" just before she saw Khon'Tor hit him over the head with a rock.

The guard crumpled at her feet. Tehya looked up in shock, and had only time to exclaim, "Adoeete? Why?" before Kweeuu came charging out of the brush past her, snarling and snapping and lunged at Khon'Tor. The two fell to the ground, a whirling bundle of fur and fury. Tehya stood back, horrified and speechless. She tried to scream, but nothing came out. She stepped back and tripped, and the last thing she remembered seeing was Khon'Tor dragging Kweeuu with him to his feet and hurling the giant grey wolf over into the brush.

When Mistok regained consciousness, he rose unsteadily to his feet and immediately searched the area. He realized Tehya was nowhere to be found. He heard Kweeuu whimpering in the bushes. The guard let out an echoing screamcall alert before running up to Kthama. As he approached, a hoard of guards came streaming out of Kthama's entrance, First Guard Awan in the lead.

"What is going on? What happened?"

The guard gasped out, "Khon'Tor's mate, Tehya, is gone. And the wolf is hurt, he is in the bushes down the path a way back."

"*What happened!*" demanded Awan.

Mistok was bent over, still trying to catch his

breath. "We took the wolf out, down this path, as usual. We were waiting for him to return. I heard someone approach and turned around—it was Khon'Tor. Just as I turned, he hit me on the head with a rock. I do not know what happened after that, but she is gone."

Awan turned to one of the guards and sent him back to find Acaraho and someone to tend to Mistok —and the wolf. To another, he said, "Stay here and wait for them, I am going farther on down the trail. Mistok, come with me in the meantime."

Mistok took Awan to the area where the struggle had taken place. They were careful not to disturb anything, knowing full well that Acaraho would want to see it as it was. Awan looked around for any evidence pointing to where Khon'Tor and Tehya might have gone. He wondered where the watcher for this area was.

Awan heard the pounding of footsteps behind him and turned to find Acaraho, Nadiwani—and Khon'Tor.

Mistok looked at the Leader, horrified.

"What happened?" Khon'Tor demanded.

Awan stood speechless. Mistok started shaking.

"By the Spirit, Awan, tell me now what the *krell* happened, or I swear—" Khon'Tor took a step toward the First Guard, his fists clenched, canines revealed in a snarl.

"You— The guard said you— Acaraho, Mistok said he was out with Tehya and the wolf when

Khon'Tor appeared and hit him over the head with a rock, knocking him out. When he came to, Tehya was gone—and so was Khon'Tor—" Awan explained.

Khon'Tor put his hands to his head and let out a heart-wrenching roar, then turned around and grabbed the first guard, easily lifting him off his feet.

"How could it have been me when I am standing here before you!" He roughly released Awan and stormed away from the group.

"Send out everyone you have, in all directions," ordered Acaraho after Awan had his balance back. "Look for any evidence of someone passing through. He has to have carried her somewhere; there is no way she would have gone willingly."

Mistok had not taken his eyes off Khon'Tor since the Leader arrived.

"You said that Khon'Tor hit you over the head with a rock?" Acaraho asked him, pointing at the Adik'Tar standing a few feet away.

"Yes, Commander," he said, glancing away from Khon'Tor for a fleeting moment. "I mean, it *was* him. The posture, everything. I do not understand."

"Mistok, it was *Akar'Tor*," said Acaraho. "He must have been practicing how to impersonate Khon'Tor. He must have had this planned for some time. Maybe not exactly this way; maybe Khon'Tor's banning him from Kthama changed his plans. But this was not a spur-of-the-moment attack, which means that Akar'Tor has taken her somewhere specific—someplace he prepared ahead of time."

Mistok nodded, just as Nadiwani arrived. She paused, and then, with a worried glance at Kweeuu, she took the guard aside to check his head wound.

"Where is Kahrok? He is the watcher for this period!" bellowed Acaraho.

"What is going on?" exclaimed Adia as she, too, arrived on the scene.

"Tehya is gone. Akar'Tor took her, impersonating Khon'Tor. Kweeuu tried to stop Akar'Tor, but—" Acaraho looked over at Khon'Tor, now staring off into the distance. He could only imagine the torment the Leader was going through.

Realizing that there was nothing more she could do, Adia turned and started tending to Kweeuu, who seemed unable to walk. She hoped he was only badly bruised, but could not be sure. Somehow, they had to get him back up to Kthama, which meant someone would have to carry him.

"I will go up and get something to calm him down; that will make it easier," said Nadiwani, now finished with Mistok.

"Make it strong; he is not going to like this," Adia called after her as Nadiwani scampered up the path toward Kthama.

When Nadiwani returned with Oh'Dar and the tincture to relax Kweeuu, the young man took the solution without hesitating, grabbed the grey wolf's muzzle, and poured it into the side of his mouth. Kweeuu tried his best to work it back out with his tongue, but Oh'Dar clamped his muzzle shut, making him swallow most of it. Adia reached her senses out to Kweeuu, trying to tell him to relax, that they were going to take care of him.

"I cannot carry him; I will need someone else to help, so we do not injure him further," said Oh'Dar.

"I will get one of the guards, but we need to wait until he is asleep," suggested Adia.

She was hoping Khon'Tor would not see the tremendous amount of blood on Kweeuu, fearing that he would think it was Tehya's.

○

The Leader was nearly out of his mind with fear and self-recrimination. *Tehya is gone. Akar has her. And we have no idea where they have gone. I cannot bear it. I cannot. It is my fault; I should have killed him when I had the chance. Surely, he would not take her back to Kayerm? Oh, could that be? If so, Haan will make sure she is safe.*

When he had done what he could, for the time being, Acaraho approached, stepping loudly enough that the Leader would know someone was there. Khon'Tor glanced back over his shoulder then away again.

"You may approach, Acaraho. I have myself a bit more under control now," he said, his voice flat.

"He has not hurt her, Khon'Tor. If he wanted to do that, we would have found her body here." Acaraho meant to be blunt; it was all that would get through to Khon'Tor while he was in that state.

"I saw the blood."

"That does not mean it is hers. If I know Kweeuu and how much he loves Tehya, Akar'Tor got the worst of it. The wolf is covered with blood, but it will be Akar'Tor's."

"How is Kweeuu?" Khon'Tor asked, still not facing the High Protector.

"We do not know. They gave him something to put him to sleep so he can be carried up to Kthama. As to where Akar'Tor might have taken Tehya, I already have guards and watchers out looking for a trail. And we will be able to see more in the morning. Come up to Kthama. There is nothing you can do here."

Khon'Tor shook his head.

"I need to be out here looking for her."

"No. Let my guards and watchers do what they do best. You will only get in the way."

Khon'Tor stared off into the distance. "Will the watchers not have seen them pass?"

"Of all the bad timing, it worked out that they were just changing shifts."

Acaraho paused before continuing, "You are no good to Tehya like this. Come and get some rest. We need you. Tehya needs you."

Adia came up to join Acaraho. She could sense

the pain and anguish radiating off of Khon'Tor. It was unbearable, even from a distance.

"They are taking Kweeuu up to the Healer's Quarters. Nadiwani and Oh'Dar are going to tend to him. Let us know what else we can do," she said softly to Acaraho. Then she looked up at him, nodded toward Khon'Tor, and shook her head as if to convey her concern over his state of mind.

"Go with your mate, Acaraho," Khon'Tor said.

"I am not leaving you. Not in this state."

"That was an order."

"*I am not leaving you in this state.*"

Khon'Tor turned to face Acaraho, "You are defying a direct order?"

"You can try me later. But I am not leaving you like this. We will find her. And when we do, the first thing she will want to see is you. She lives for you just as much as you live for her. I know you are suffering. I know you are worried to death because I would also be. But if the situation were reversed, you would be telling me the same thing. You cannot give up on her."

"How dare you say I am giving up on her. And who the *krell* are you to tell me what I should or should not do?" shouted Khon'Tor, his eyes narrowed.

"I am your High Protector. I am one of your Circle of Council, you just said so yesterday. And believe it or not, I am on your side."

"If you were truly on my side, you would leave me alone."

"No."

"Leave! Or I will *make* you!"

"I will not leave you, Khon'Tor."

Khon'Tor roared, charged Acaraho, and tackled him to the ground, enraged. The two giants rolled in the dirt, each trying to gain a stronghold; first, Acaraho took the advantage, and then Khon'Tor. Others in the distance heard the snarling and froze, knowing they could not intervene. Somehow, Acaraho managed to get Khon'Tor on the ground with his arm behind his back and leaned his full weight against the Leader to keep him pinned.

Khon'Tor roared in frustration, and Acaraho felt the Leader's body start to shake as rage turned to heartbreak. After a moment, the High Protector released Khon'Tor's arm and helped him sit up. Acaraho then waved the others back and sat with an arm around the Leader's shoulders. Khon'Tor, beyond shame, broke down, his body wracked with sobs.

"Listen to me. We are going to find her, Khon'Tor. I promise. She is smart. You *know* how smart she is. Tehya will figure out how to survive. And she knows we will be looking for her, that we will be doing everything we can to find her."

"I need to be out there looking too," he repeated.

"No, you do not. Let my guards do their jobs. Tromping blindly around out there is not going to help anything. When you are ready, we should go up and check in with the others."

The two giants sat alone together a while. Finally, Khon'Tor conceded, and they rose. Walking silently side-by-side, they made their way up to Kthama.

CHAPTER 10

When Tehya awoke, she had no idea where she was. The last thing she remembered was Khon'Tor attacking the guard and then the fight with Kweeuu. *Had it been a nightmare? Was she home back in their quarters?* She was lying on something soft, but it was dark, and she could not quite get her bearings. She realized that Khon'Tor was right there beside her, and she relaxed and sighed. *It was just a bad dream. But it had been so real.*

She rolled over and put an arm over Khon'Tor's side. Something was not right. For one thing, he was on the wrong side. He never slept on her right because he was left-handed. She sat up and tried to clear her head, just as the figure next to her also sat up. In the dim light, it looked like Khon'Tor, but in her spirit, she could feel the truth, and her hand flew to her mouth in horror.

"Akar'Tor! Where am I? *What have you done?*"

"Sssh, Tehya. Everything is alright now. You are here with me, where you belong."

Her hand went immediately to her belly, checking that everything was alright with her offspring. Wherever they were, Akar'Tor must have carried her after she had fallen, and she was relieved that nothing was amiss as far as she could tell.

"You cannot do this. You have to let me go," she said, the reality of the situation now becoming clear.

"You do not understand. I did this for you—for us. You are safe now. He will never touch you again. I have planned this a long time; when it gets light enough, I will show you. I have everything prepared."

Her blood ran cold. *He is insane. He has taken me prisoner under some delusion that we belong together. Even after what I said to him in front of everyone, in the Great Chamber—*

Tehya tried to think, but her head was still fuzzy. She did not know how long she had been passed out or how far they had traveled, but she was sure that by now, they would have realized she was missing. She was worried about Kweeuu—afraid that Akar'Tor had killed him when he threw the wolf against the hillside. Mistok had also been hurt.

She lay back down, turning away from Akar'Tor. *I do not know what he is thinking, but he had better not touch me. Surely he would not; he knows I am with offspring.*

Akar'Tor covered her up with a deer hide he had taken from Kayerm. "You rest now. In the morning, I will show you everything—you will see!"

Tehya lay there as still as she could, but there was no way she could go to sleep. She prayed to the Great Mother that Kweeuu and Mistok were alright and that Khon'Tor would find her before her offspring was born.

Nadiwani had sent Mistok back to his quarters with a bandage and strict instructions to rest. She and Adia were confident that he would recover well.

Khon'Tor had returned to Kthama and was now in the work area with Oh'Dar and the three Healers.

Oh'Dar was leaning over the worktable, cleaning the blood off Kweeuu's fur, and looking for wounds. "So far, I do not see any punctures or reasons for all the blood. And from the amount around his muzzle, I will guarantee that it is Akar'Tor's. Kweeuu seems to have inflicted quite a few solid bites." Oh'Dar made sure to stress that it was Akar'Tor's blood and imply that there was no chance it could be Tehya's.

"Acaraho has everyone available out looking for tracks, drops of blood, anything that would indicate where he took her," said Adia.

Khon'Tor stood unmoving, not saying a word.

Urilla Wuti closed her eyes, then opened them and looked at Khon'Tor. She did not want to discuss it here in front of Oh'Dar as he did not know about the other Healer abilities—but Khon'Tor was in such a state that she did not feel it prudent to wait for a more private moment.

"Khon'Tor. Your offspring is fine. And that means Tehya is as well."

Khon'Tor looked at her, for the first time returning to the current world from wherever his thoughts had taken him.

"You can tell that?"

"I can tell you they both are alright. At least physically."

"What do you mean *at least physically*? *Is Tehya hurt*?" Khon'Tor exclaimed.

"It means that I can tell they are physically unharmed, though Tehya is under a great deal of mental and emotional stress. But that is to be expected," Urilla Wuti clarified.

Khon'Tor let out a long sigh. *I am not even going to ask how she knows.*

"I have known Tehya all her life, Khon'Tor. I know her better than anyone—maybe even you. She is smart. She is resourceful. She is under duress, of course, but she will not just roll over and let this happen to her. She is easygoing, but when backed into a corner, she will fight for herself and your offspring. If I know her, Tehya is already thinking of a way to escape. She loves you more than you can possibly understand. If there is any opportunity, she will find her way back to you."

Adia could feel the self-blame and recrimination emanating from Khon'Tor. It was so strong that she had to move a few feet away. For some reason, her seventh sense seemed lately to be augmented, though she had no idea why.

"I am going to my quarters. Let me know about the wolf."

After he was gone, Adia turned to the others.

"His state of mind is not good. He is blaming himself for all this. I am deeply worried about him."

"I sense it too," said Urilla Wuti. "He should not be left alone at this time."

"Not much we can do about that, except check in on him regularly until he has a fit about it, which he will," said Nadiwani.

"I will do it," offered Oh'Dar. "Perhaps he will take it better from a male."

"How is Kweeuu?"

"I need someone to set him down on the floor now. I have done all I can to clean him up. From what I can tell, nothing is broken, though I do not know how. But he is clearly bruised and going to be hurting for some time yet. Willow bark might ease some of his discomfort," Oh'Dar said.

Adia summoned the guard who was stationed outside, more a messenger than a protector, and had him help move Kweeuu onto his mat, earlier retrieved from the Leader's Quarters.

Though it was unnecessary, Oh'Dar could not

resist covering him up, stroking his head and speaking comforting words to the wolf.

"You did well, Kweeuu. You tried to protect her. Now just rest and heal. Rest and heal."

Khon'Tor went back to his quarters. He entered the room and stopped. He remembered a time before when she was not there, and it had the same feeling of overwhelming emptiness. Discarded wrappings were crumpled in a heap by her side of the sleeping mat, one of the few habits he found annoying and something he had admonished her before for doing. *"Why do you just leave them where you take them off, female?"*

Now he regretted ever mentioning it. The necklace he had made for Tehya was in its place on her personal table with her other personal items. Reminders were everywhere, and as before, Khon'Tor could not stand being there without her.

How could I have let this happen? She depended on me to protect her, and I failed. She is alone and at his mercy. Why, why, why, did I not kill Akar when I had the chance? If I had, she would still be here with me, safe in my arms.

Khon'Tor took one last look around the room and left. In anguish, he walked the tunnels of Kthama for the next few hours.

Somehow, Tehya did doze off despite her troubled state. When she awoke, she was cold and alone. She struggled up from the sleeping mat, wrapping the soft hide around her for warmth. She was glad she had her warm deer hide wrappings and fur boots on, or she would have been colder still.

The room she was in was not very large, with fairly low ceilings. The entrance was blocked by a huge boulder. There was room for the sleeping area, some supplies in a corner, and stacked toward the front, a pile of wood for a small fire. Tehya wished it was lit. She looked around and found the flint and quartz stones, but with no kindling, she knew she would not be able to get it started. She returned to the sleeping mat and huddled under the hide, trying to stay warm.

Before too long, the scraping of the boulder brought her out of her daze. Akar'Tor had returned with a bundle of twigs, leaves, and dried grass. She was grateful to see them and ached for the warmth of a fire.

He walked over and dumped his collection next to the firewood, never taking his eyes off her. Tehya made a point not to look at the open entrance—she knew she would never make it in time and did not want to anger him.

Akar'Tor then pulled the boulder back in place

over the entrance, leaving enough of a gap for light to enter.

He sorted the materials and went about making a fire. As soon as it was lit, Tehya moved over to sit next to it, even though it meant getting closer to Akar'Tor.

"Are you cold?" he asked.

"Yes. I am cold. I do not have your covering, Akar'Tor," she said, realizing that it had come out more accusatory than she intended. "Why have you taken me prisoner? I want to go home. Please. I am carrying an offspring; surely, you can tell that?"

"Yes, I know. But do not worry, I will take care of it. Then we can make our own," he said matter-of-factly, staring at her swollen belly.

Take care of it? A cold shiver went through her soul. She pushed down the panic rising inside her.

"Oh, no, Akar, I will take care of it; you do not have to bother, I am looking forward to it," she said, intentionally misconstruing his meaning.

"No. I mean, I will get rid of it. We do not need it. I do not want you fussing over it and distracted by it. I have seen my mother with Kalli; an offling takes up a lot of time, and we have our own lives to get on with. Do not worry; I will put my own seed in you, and then you can play with that one when it comes out. I have seen it done; I know how it works."

By the Mother, he is either insane or addled. He is going to kill my offspring. I have to get out of here. But how? I cannot move that boulder, and I cannot overpower him. She looked around the cave for something to use as a weapon but could see nothing sturdy enough.

"What are you looking for?" he asked.

"I am hungry. Do you have anything to eat in here?" she asked.

"Over there in the corner, there is some dried meat and some hazelnuts. And a gourd of water."

She moved to where he had indicated, still holding the deer hide around her. She picked through the supplies, realizing there was not enough here to last for more than a few days. She tried to calm her mind; if only she knew exactly when the offspring was due and how much time she had to make a plan to escape.

They will be looking for me, but do they even have any idea where to start? I cannot depend on them to find me. I somehow, on my own, have to save myself and my daughter. If I can gain his trust, perhaps he will drop his guard, and that will be my chance. But I cannot outrun him—especially not in this condition.

Tehya stayed huddled in the corner, thinking and eating until the cold drove her back to the fire and Akar'Tor. As she sat soaking up the heat, she decided on a plan.

"Thank you for making the fire; it is very welcoming."

"I am glad you like it. I did this all for you, Tehya. For us."

"It is a nice little place. Did it take you long to find?"

"I knew of it earlier; I used to come here and play when I was growing up."

"What did you play? With friends?"

"No, I did not have any friends. Well, maybe one. I did not fit in, and the others were so much stronger than me, I could not join in their games. I used to come and pretend this was another Kayerm only *I* was the Leader, not my father—not Haan."

"I am sure you would be a great Leader, Akar'-Tor," she said. *What am I doing?* But she answered her own question. *What I must.*

Akar'Tor's head snapped in her direction, "Yes, I would be. And I will be—someday I will lead the People of the High Rocks. You will see. They will all see."

"Akar, I need to go outside. It has been all night if you know what I mean?"

"Alright. But do not try to get away. I do not want to hurt you, Tehya," and he got up, moved the boulder, and followed her outside.

Once outside, her eyes moved slowly across the horizon, looking for some clue to where they were. She found a set of bushes not far off the path and asked Akar'Tor to wait where he was. To her surprise, he gave her the privacy she needed.

On the way back, she looked around again but could find nothing that gave away their location.

She carefully lowered herself to sit back down next to the fire. To her horror, he came and sat behind her, straddling her with his thighs as he had seen Khon'Tor do. She suppressed a shudder, and her heart started pounding in fear. He wrapped his arms around her and tried to get her to lean back into him, again mimicking Khon'Tor's common embrace of her.

Tehya forced herself to go along, squeezing her eyes shut so she would not lash out and attack him. *Please, Great Spirit; please do not let him try to mate me. I could not bear it. Please. Surely, he will not, not with my condition.*

Akar'Tor leaned forward and whispered in her ear, "How long before your offling is born Tehya? I cannot wait to be with you. I will make you forget all about my father."

She could feel him responding to the pressure of her body pressed against him. Tears rolled down her cheeks, and she inched her hand up to wipe them away before he could tell. *Great Mother, forgive me.* She was glad he could not see her face.

"I want only you, Tehya. He has no right to be with you. He is too old. You belong with me; I am glad you are seeing it now." He started to run his hands up and down her arms, then wrapped his around her. He nuzzled his face into her neck. Her skin crawled, and she shuddered.

"Thank you for rescuing me, Akar. And for the fire. It is cold in here. Are there any more hides or wrappings?" Anything to try to change his focus.

"No, but I can perhaps get some more from Kayerm."

So we are not too far from Kayerm. I wonder if Haan knows of this place? I wonder if they have told Haan that Akar'Tor has taken me?

"It would be very sweet if you could. And if we put some stones around the fire, they would pick up the heat and send it back out into the room even after the fire is out. Do your people not do that at Kayerm?"

Akar'Tor thought for a moment and remembered. "You are correct. I knew something did not look right. I will collect some. I want you to be happy here."

"I am sure I will be, Akar; I am with you, am I not?" The words sliced through her soul as she said them. She wanted to keep him talking, to keep his mind off his state of arousal. She looked down at his legs and arms wrapped around her and noticed a lot of blood.

"Akar, you are hurt," she said.

"That *PetaQ* wolf bit me. He was all over me. It was all I could do to get him off."

"Let me get some water and clean up your wounds; you do not want them to get infected," she offered. *Anything to get out of his embrace before he forgets I am seeded or stops caring. Does he even know how to mate? Do they have an Ashwea Tare?*

Tehya extracted herself from between his legs, went over to the water bowl, and looked around for some little piece of material. Finding nothing, she tried tearing a piece off the deer hide.

"I do not suppose you have a cutting blade?"

"No," he said.

She took hold of the hem of the gauzy under-sheath she wore beneath the buckskin, and tore a piece off, careful not to take too much. She brought the water over and started carefully cleaning the blood off his legs and arms. He winced with each touch.

"Some of these are deep puncture wounds, Akar. Do you have a Healer back at Kayerm?"

"It will be alright. I am not worried about them," he said.

She finished cleaning him, rinsed out the rag, and hung it on a piece of rock that protruded near the ceiling. Then she took a spot back at the fire across from him. *I am so hungry. I wonder how long I have been missing. Khon'Tor must be out of his mind by now with worry. Oh, how I wish I could let him know I am alright, that I am alive and our offspring is too —so far.*

Early the next morning, Acaraho was receiving the reports from the search groups when Khon'Tor came up. "So far, we have found nothing. He crossed at the river or walked down along the river bed; we are not sure. The rain has made tracking him difficult," he explained, then continued.

"I cannot sit and do nothing, despite what you

say. I am going to the valley to leave the signal for contact," Khon'Tor announced.

"I will go with you."

They set off down the path to the valley where Acaraho had been told to make the tree breaks. Khon'Tor was silent the entire journey, and Acaraho did not press him to talk.

"Here, these are the two locusts we mark. I do not know if they have watchers here all the time, or they just check this area locally. But it seems they know within a day or two when we have asked for contact."

"*Tehya may not have a day or two*," said Khon'Tor and stormed over to one of the larger trees and positioned himself against it. He placed his hands on the trunk, braced his feet, and with all his strength, *pushed*. With a loud *crack*, the tree's taproot severed, and the trunk started to pull up from the ground. He pushed again, and the root ball came farther up and finally out, the tree now resting at an angle. Finally, with one last great effort, he pushed the huge tree over, and it went toppling down, landing on the valley floor with an earsplitting and ground-shaking thump, the forest protesting as the massive tree came to rest. Then Khon'Tor took a deep breath and roared as loud as he could "Haaaaannnnnnnn!"

Acaraho stood transfixed at the display of sheer power. *Well, that ought to do it.*

Minutes passed. Khon'Tor listened to the continuing silence. "Did you hear that?"

"No."

"Exactly. Someone is here. It is too quiet. Even after the tree crash, the sounds should have returned. We will wait a while longer. No doubt Haan or one of his messengers will be along very shortly."

Khon'Tor was exactly right. In no time, one of the Sarnonn came out, apparently from nowhere. Acaraho thought he recognized him as one he had seen before.

"You want to talk to the Adik'Tar Haan?"

"Yes. It is important. Now," said Khon'Tor.

The Sarnonn looked perplexed; he clearly did not know what to do. He could not take them to Kayerm, but the urgency of the situation and the ongoing prohibition about contact with the Akassa threw him.

"Please go and tell Haan to come now. Tell him it is critically urgent," said Acaraho.

The Sarnonn moved away quickly, looking back over his shoulder at them.

They waited for some time, but it was not that long before he returned with Haan. Acaraho noted this and realized that possibly Kayerm was closer than they thought, though he could not be sure what a Sarnonn's fastest running speed was.

"What is wrong, Khon'Tor, Acaraho?" asked Haan, concern in his voice.

"Tehya is gone. Akar'Tor has her," said Acaraho. "One of the guards with her thought it was Khon'Tor, but he was with us at the time. It had to be Akar'Tor impersonating him."

Haan frowned and closed his eyes and shook his head.

"Do you know where he could have taken her?" asked Khon'Tor.

"No. I do not. But we will search. And I will ask his mother; she may know," Haan said. "He has not come home for several days."

"Haan, she is with offspring, and it is due—*any day,*" Acaraho added.

"We will do our best to find them," he said.

"If he hurts her—" Khon'Tor blurted out, but, given the presence of Haan, he regretted the threat the moment he had spoken.

"I do not believe he will harm her. But the offling —*that I do not know.* I am sorry. I will immediately assemble help, and we will start looking straight away."

And Haan turned back the way he had come.

Khon'Tor's knees almost buckled. With the thoughts of Tehya at Akar'Tor's mercy, he had forgotten about how soon the offspring was due.

He fell to his knees and put his head in his hands.

"Khon'Tor," said Acaraho.

"Leave me. Go back. I will return later," he said, not looking up.

This time, Acaraho did as Khon'Tor asked; the High Protector had to get back to Kthama to see if there was any news.

Khon'Tor was beside himself. *Our offspring. Tehya's offspring. I pray Haan is right, that he will not hurt her—it is she he wants. But he will not want my offspring around. We have to find her soon; we have to.*

Khon'Tor stayed there alone for some time, unmoving. Finally, he headed back to Kthama.

Back in the cave, Tehya's ears pricked up. She thought she had heard something crashing heavily to the ground and then what sounded like a male howl of anguish. She looked over at Akar'Tor, who was sitting absentmindedly by the fire. *Akar'Tor doesn't act like he heard anything. It was so far away. And what was it? There were no words that I could hear. No, it is just my imagination. I want to go home so badly that I am hearing things now. Oh, please, dear Mother, please let me get home. Please save my offspring.*

Haan returned to Kayerm as quickly as possible. Now he knew what Akar'Tor had been working on during the day. His son had been preparing a place to hide Tehya. Haan headed straight to find Hakani, who looked up as he stormed into their living quarters.

"I have just met with Khon'Tor and Acaraho. Akar has stolen Tehya, and no one knows where he has taken her. All this time he has been gone, he has no doubt been making a place to keep her. Do you have any idea where that could be?"

Hakani stopped what she was doing. "How do they know it was Akar?" she said, her voice shaking.

"One of the guards was with her when Akar attacked him. The guard thought it was Khon'Tor, but it wasn't."

Akar has Tehya? This has gotten out of hand. Would he hurt her? I do not think so. But it seems I do not know him anymore, so he might. "Is Tehya still with offspring?"

"Yes, and she is due any time now."

Hakani shook her head. *What have I done? I turned Akar against his natural father. My hatred of Khon'Tor has brought this down on our heads. If Akar harms that offspring, Khon'Tor will move the stars and Etera to get revenge. This will be the end of any peace between our people. And there goes any hope of living at Kthama again. Where could he have taken her?*

"He has to have prepared a place for them to stay. There is no way they are out in the open; they would be found too easily." Then she paused. "I have an idea where he might be."

"Where? *Where?*"

"When he was old enough to play on his own, there was a cave he used to play in. If you remember, he had only one friend, Inhrah, so he often played by himself. It is not too far; it is between here and the valley where you meet Khon'Tor and Acaraho."

"Can you find it?"

"I think so," she said, still preoccupied with visions of what would happen if Akar'Tor harmed Tehya or her offling.

Haan thought for a moment. "I am going to find Inhrah. He and Akar still have some kind of friendship, and it may come in handy. In the meantime, get someone to watch Kalli. We need to leave at first light."

When Khon'Tor got back to Kthama, the searchers were all still out. Not finding Acaraho, he went to his quarters. He noticed the door ajar, though the guard was still in place. He went in to find Oh'Dar sitting at the work table.

"I am sorry, Khon'Tor. I did not intend to enter your quarters uninvited. Forgive me, but I could not keep him out of here—" He motioned to where Kweeuu was lying on Tehya's side of the sleeping mat.

"I tried and tried, but he just would not obey. He literally dragged himself; it is as if he has to be here," Oh'Dar explained.

Khon'Tor raised a hand, "It is fine. He can stay. He loves her too."

"Can I do anything for you?" asked Oh'Dar.

"No, thank you. Except to pray. Pray that we find

her. Pray that the offspring is alright. That you could do."

"I will Khon'Tor. I promise," and with that Oh'Dar turned to leave, but before he left, he turned back, "I brought you a present from the Waschini world. It is a knife, with what they call a metal blade. I know you do not need a weapon, but I thought you could appreciate the workmanship."

Khon'Tor nodded, and then Oh'Dar placed the gift on the workspace and left.

Khon'Tor looked down at the giant grey wolf on his mate's side of the bed. Somehow Kweeuu's presence was comforting to him. Too tired to care about eating, or anything else, he lay down next to Kweeuu and put an arm over him. Kweeuu whimpered, but within moments was asleep again. Khon'Tor lay awake most of the night, picturing what he would do to Akar'Tor if the young male were not Haan's son.

Tehya found a sharp stone in one of the corners and started making a mark for each day she was there, taking care only to do it when Akar'Tor was away. It seemed as if it had rained for days. She was also very hungry. She started worrying about whether her offspring was getting enough nourishment from the meager diet Akar'Tor was providing. Each day that passed brought her closer to her delivery, and she was not sure how long she had been unconscious before she first woke up and found herself there.

I am running out of time. I have to find a way to escape.

It was getting harder to pretend she was happy there. She knew Akar'Tor trusted her a little bit more each day. But the pressure of the passing time was wearing her down. It was all she could do not to attack him in his sleep, but she could not escape as long as the huge boulder was in place. And if she did manage to get out, she was so heavy with her offspring that she could barely run. So she was steeling herself to wait and pray that an opportunity presented itself. *Whenever I make my move, the boulder has to be away from the door. I cannot get out otherwise.*

"When is that thing going to come out of you?" he asked

She wanted to scream, "*It is not a thing!*" Instead, she replied, "I do not know exactly."

"Can you make it come out sooner? Like they did with my mother? I am tired of this waiting for us to get on with our lives," he said.

"No, no, Akar, I cannot. She needs to stay inside me as long as she can. She is not ready yet. She is a little offspring. Just a little offspring, Akar, no threat to us," and she started to cry.

"See, it upsets you to even talk about it. The sooner I get rid of it, the better," and he jabbed a stick into the fire, making the embers flare.

"I do not want you to get rid of it, Akar. I want to keep my little one." She was breaking down.

"Stop crying. It will be over and done with soon."

"What are you going to do?" she sobbed.

"The same thing my father did to my mother, throw it into the Great River to drown."

Tehya sobbed openly.

"Stop it. *Stop it*!" he yelled. "Why do you care about that thing? After what Khon'Tor did to the Healer Adia, to my mother, forcing offling into them against their will! Why do you want it? You should want to be rid of it too! *I do not like it when you are like this!*"

Tehya put her hands over her face to try and muffle her crying, and she struggled up and went to squat in the farthest corner of the cave. *He is making up accusations against Khon'Tor to turn me to his side. Great Mother, where are you? Why do you not help me? Please!*

Akar'Tor went back to stirring the fire. Tehya could only bear to stay in the cold corner so long and finally had to return to its heat. She took a place across from her captor, trying to avoid any chance of physical contact while being close to the warmth.

She looked across at Akar'Tor, who was lit by the firelight. She could see the wounds on his legs.

"Akar, your wounds do not look good. Do they hurt?"

"I try not to think about them. Yes, they hurt a lot."

She squinted, trying to see better from where she was. "They look infected."

"I do not know. Maybe." Akar'Tor stared at her, eyes narrowed. She saw him run his gaze over her.

He is becoming very irritable, and no doubt, his wounds hurt. Something must happen soon, before his patience breaks.

Oh'Dar's thoughts kept going back to Kweeuu, dragging himself down the tunnels to Khon'Tor's quarters, where the wolf had spent most of his time with Tehya.

Kweeuu tracked me all the way to Shadow Ridge. It probably took him a while, but he did it. Could he not also track Tehya? They said Akar'Tor crossed the river—I am sure to make us lose his trail. But it could not have been the trail that led Kweeuu to me at Shadow Ridge—I think it had something to do with the natural bond between us. Maybe the bond between him and Tehya would be enough for Kweeuu to find her too.

Oh'Dar went to find his father. Before interrupting, he impatiently let Acaraho's conversation with the guards die down.

"I have an idea, Father," he said. Acaraho turned his attention to his son and excused himself from the circle.

"What is it, son? Is it about Tehya?"

"Remember why I came back to Kthama the first

time? Kweeuu had tracked me to Shadow Ridge, and I came back to bring him home."

Acaraho immediately caught on, "And you think he might be able to find Tehya?"

"Yes. Yes, I do. But he has to be strong enough to make it all the way. If he collapses, we are no better off. And, though I know Tehya's life and that of her offspring are important, I do not want to lose him—and with no result." said Oh'Dar.

Acaraho noticed Oh'Dar's emotional response. *He has such a good, caring heart. Like his mother, Adia, even though they are not of the same blood.* "Of course. When do you think Kweeuu would be strong enough? We are racing against time."

"I will check him out now and let you know."

"I will come with you." And the two males headed fo__r Khon'Tor's quarters.

As they approached, the guard told them that Khon'Tor had already left Kthama.

Rok, thought Acaraho. *We might have a chance at finding her, and Khon'Tor is out roaming around the Great Spirit knows where! He is the first person she will want to see if we find her. When we find her.*

They went in to find Kweeuu still on Tehya's side of the bed. He lifted his head and wagged his huge tail as he saw them approach.

"How are you doing?" Oh'Dar asked. Kweeuu panted, which always made him look as if he was smiling, and wagged his tail some more. Then he put his head back down.

Oh'Dar went over the wolf's body, checking. "His wounds are closing nicely. I think he is just bruised. Why not take him outside and see how he does; he probably needs to go out anyway."

When they took Kweeuu outside, he moved a little slower than usual but did not seem to be in too much pain—though it was hard to tell with animals because they did not always show how they were hurting.

Kweeuu started down the path to where Tehya had been seen last, not to the place they had trained him to use. Oh'Dar called him back. Kweeuu stopped, turned to look at him and whimpered.

"Could this work?" asked Acaraho.

"I say it is worth a try. If Kweeuu had not found me at Shadow Ridge, I would not have thought of it," said Oh'Dar.

"You will have to go with him, but you cannot go alone; let me grab some help. Is there anything else we need to take? Healing supplies?"

Oh'Dar became silent. "Yes. I need to get a satchel of supplies, in case she needs medical attention— Or —" and he did not finish the sentence. "But Kweeuu is not going to come back inside, and I should stay here, so he does not take off without us."

"Tell me what you need, and I will ask your mother to gather it up."

Adia was hopeful at hearing their plan. She put everything together in her own worn satchel, the one she always used, the one in which she had carried Oh'Dar home so long ago.

Soon Acaraho was back with the satchel and a guard. Oh'Dar noticed the guard was armed with a spear.

"Here we go."

Had Kweeuu not been bruised and sore, they would never have kept up with him. He led them to the Great River and down the banks. The wolf could not pick up a scent but seemed still to have an idea where to go, which confirmed for Oh'Dar that he was tracking her on a different level. Finally, Kweeuu crossed the icy cold river, everyone suffering in their aversion to water, except for Oh'Dar.

Along the way, Oh'Dar gave Kweeuu a tincture for pain to make it easier for him.

Eventually, they came to the valley where Khon'Tor had toppled the tree to contact Haan, the massive root ball still sticking straight out of the ground.

"What in Etera? How did that fall over? It is not even rotted," said Oh'Dar.

"It did not fall. Khon'Tor pushed it over to get the Sarnonns' attention. Needless to say, it was effective. Haan is out looking as well, I am sure," Acaraho explained.

Some distance away, Haan, Hakani, and Inhrah were indeed also out looking for Akar'Tor and Tehya.

Hakani tried to remember how to get to the cave. Years ago, she had been there numerous times to check on him, though he would never let her stay there as she was not *part of this world*, he used to say. It was so long ago; she remembered the general area but not the exact location. She was scanning the edge of the mountain that housed Kayerm, looking for the opening to the cave. The closer she got, the better she remembered where it should be, but she had always been dependent on a gaping hole to locate it.

"It should be along here. I do not know why I cannot find it. Brush must have grown over the entrance," she said as they stamped their way through the thick grasses.

Oh'Dar, Acaraho, the guard, and Kweeuu were making their way to the same place, but from the opposite direction.

CHAPTER 11

As the guard had informed Acaraho, Khon'Tor had indeed left Kthama early, well before daybreak. He knew it was probably useless, but he walked around, trying to picture where Tehya was, how she was doing. He prayed to the Great Spirit, the One who had created Etera and who provided for them. As he walked, his prayers became thoughts and reflection.

This is my fault. There is no other way to look at it. If I had not been consumed with power, prideful about being the Adoeete, Leader of the largest community in the People in the region—none of this would have happened. I resented Adia from the beginning as if it was her fault that she was chosen to be Healer and was therefore out of my reach. I had no idea that Hakani knew Adia was my First Choice, or that it would eat at her all those years the way it did. Perhaps I could have dealt with Hakani's rejection of me differently. Perhaps I could have made more of an effort to figure out what was wrong and made amends. Or if I had not chosen Hakani in my haste to protect my pride after Adia was named Healer— I do not know how to figure it all out. I only know that now, my sweet Tehya, the mate I never dreamed I would have or deserve, is at the mercy of my son who hates me. A son seeded in contempt and brewed in a stew of hatred.

The longer he walked, the more Khon'Tor's self-repudiation grew.

Hakani, surviving all those years, then turning up alive, only to bring more trouble into my life, her hatred and resentment of me now also living in our offspring. How ironic that Akar'Tor looks just like me. This is the punishment I knew would come one day; this is the circle of life turning back on me for the crimes and evils I committed. I took the Healer Without Her Consent. A maiden dedicated to the welfare of the community that I was charged with protecting. I took from her what no male had the right. And the others. What has happened to them? Do they also secretly hate me? Or have they found a way to make peace with my wrongdoings? Awan's mate is one of them, living in my very own community.

Khon'Tor continued walking the winding paths around Kthama.

But Tehya is innocent; she has done nothing wrong. She could not help that I chose her. Her only mistake was in giving me her heart. I never deserved love, and I am lucky to have been with her the short time I have. Why should she pay for my abominable acts? Perhaps that is it. Everything I did, every wrong I committed—I was never punished for any of it. Instead, innocents around me, like Adia, like Tehya, even Nootau and Nimida, are paying for my wrongdoing. The Great Spirit is exacting from them the payment that was mine to make.

With no one to challenge his thoughts, Khon'Tor started down a dead-end path into darkness.

Inside the cave, huddled for warmth under the meager pelt, Tehya felt her offspring move. She placed her hand on her belly and said a prayer. Tears welled in her eyes. She was grateful that Akar'Tor was napping, because only then could she let out her grief and anguish. Suddenly, Tehya felt a gush and realized her water cradle had broken.

Please, Great Mother. My offspring is going to come —not here, please, oh please. Please save her; she is innocent, and she deserves a chance at life. You cannot let her die at the hands of this twisted monster. He is insane!

Tehya moved carefully, terrified that Akar'Tor would wake before she could clean up. She quietly mopped up the evidence with the now dry piece of fabric she had used to tend Akar'Tor's wounds.

Just as she finished, Tehya thought she heard something in the distance. She struggled to her feet and moved toward the boulder, wondering if she might see anything through the cracks. Her stirring woke Akar'Tor, who lifted his head, his voice gruff, "What are you doing?"

"I thought I heard something, that is all," *What does he think? Surely, he knows I cannot move this giant rock and get away.*

"What did you hear?"

"I do not know, but something definitely unusual." She was not going to tell him that she thought perhaps it was the howl of a coyote or wolf. *Let him worry about something for a change.*

Haan and his crew had heard it too. It sounded like a wolf to them.

Tehya moved from the doorway as Akar'Tor got up from the mat and came over to look. Not being able to see anything, he started to move the boulder away.

Time was running out. She knew her offspring was going to be born soon. Tehya saw her chance. With difficulty, she leaned over and picked up one of the stones that she had been slowly and patiently easing away from the flames so it would not be as hot as the others and scorch her hands—waiting for just such an opportunity.

Just as Akar'Tor moved the boulder from the opening, Tehya grabbed the rock and smashed it against the back of his head.

He groaned and collapsed to the ground. He was still conscious, though, but Tehya was afraid to hit him over the head again for fear of killing him.

Moaning, Akar'Tor reached for her ankle, and she stepped back into the cave, barely evading his grasp. He crawled toward her, but Tehya had an idea.

She stepped farther back into the cave, and Akar'Tor continued to drag himself toward her. She bit her lip and raised the rock again, this time hurling it directly down on the most infected part of his right leg.

Smack!

Akar'Tor howled in pain and grabbed his leg, curling into a ball. Tehya had lured him far enough into the back of the cave that she could get past him. She dropped the rock and ran out through the gap he had made when he moved the boulder aside.

Hakani saw the movement of the stone from the doorway.

"There!" she pointed. They quickly turned and headed through the forest to the place Hakani had indicated.

From the other direction, Kweeuu had indeed howled. He had picked up a clean, fresh scent, and his excitement could not be contained. They followed him as quickly as they could—coming around the corner just in time to hear Akar'Tor's painful cry and see Tehya fleeing from the opening as fast as she could.

Within moments they were with her. Tehya ran into Oh'Dar's arms, almost knocking him over.

"By the Mother! Kweeuu found you!" he exclaimed.

"Where were you, Tehya? And where is Akar'-Tor?" Acaraho shouted.

"Back there, in a cave. That is where he has kept

me all this time," and she pointed back to the opening through which she had just escaped.

"Did he hurt you?" Acaraho asked, fearing the worst but needing to know.

"No. But he was planning to kill my offspring after she was born, and she is now about to come. Oh, I cannot believe you are here. Where is Khon'-Tor?" she gasped, as Oh'Dar tried to hold her upright.

Acaraho noticed motion from the other direction and saw Haan, Hakani, and another Sarnonn coming their way.

"You have her!" shouted Haan as they closed the distance.

"Where is Akar'Tor?" called out Hakani.

Acaraho pointed to the cave opening that was a short distance away. Hakani was already headed for the entrance. Acaraho wanted to fetch Akar'Tor and drag him back to Kthama for Khon'Tor to deal with as he saw fit, but realized that because Akar'Tor was Haan's son, his punishment should fall to the Sarnonn Leader. And the last thing Tehya needed on their journey home was any more of Akar'Tor's presence.

Haan bounded over to see how Tehya was.

"Did he hurt you? Are you and the offspring alright?" he asked.

"No, he did not hurt me. So far, we are alright, but the offspring is going to be born soon," she explained. "My water cradle broke."

Amid all the commotion, Kweeuu was trying to get Tehya's attention, but Oh'Dar ordered him down.

She noticed, disengaged from Oh'Dar, and somehow managed to bend over enough to hug the wolf around his strong neck.

"Oh, Kweeuu. Thank you. Thank you for finding me. You are such a good wolf."

By now, Hakani had found the entrance and saw Akar'Tor inside, lying on the ground writhing in pain. "Akar!"

"Mama! Where is Tehya? Get her for me. Please!"

"No, Akar. You cannot keep Tehya captive! That is wrong. She is not your mate; she belongs to Khon'Tor."

"No. *No*. She belongs to me; why are you not helping?"

"I *am* trying to help you. You must see that what you did is wrong."

"No!" he shouted and lashed out at her, his nails scratching her shins and drawing blood.

"Get away from me. I hate you. I thought you cared about me. Get out!" he shouted.

"Akar, it is me, it is your mother!"

"I do not care because you do not care about me. Leave, or I will make you," he cried.

Hakani realized she could not help Akar'Tor, not like he was.

"I will send Inhrah to get Artadel the Healer to come and tend to you. We will be back as soon as we can."

"Do not bother. I can take care of myself. I do not need anyone, and I do not need you anymore. I am sorry I was ever born. If you come back, it is at your own risk, I am warning you," he growled.

Hakani looked at her son who was still overcome with pain. *Is he mad? Is his mind warped? Did I do this to him? He was not like this when he was born. I have ruined his life as well as my own. Whose will I ruin next —Kalli's?*

Outside, Haan saw Hakani coming to join them.

Oh'Dar spoke up. "Haan, we have to get Tehya back to Kthama. My father could carry her, but please, you could easily hold her with less risk of harming her or her offspring."

Haan looked back at them and down at little Tehya. He reached over and gently picked her up, making an expansive place for her in his folded arms. She curled against his chest, taking comfort from the warmth and thick fur. She could feel and hear the beating of his huge heart, and for the first time in days, she was finally warm again.

Hakani had caught up.

"We are taking her back to Kthama. How is Akar?"

"He is out of his mind. I truly think he is sick in the head, Haan. I tried to help him, and he attacked me," she said, pointing to the blood now beading on her legs.

Hakani turned to Inhrah and said, "Go back to Kayerm and bring Artadel and supplies. He is hurt and has multiple wounds that look infected. He said he did not want help, but clearly, he needs it."

Tehya answered from her place supported by Haan's huge arms, "I tended to his wounds as much as he would let me; they are definitely infected, and they cover his legs." Then she put her head down and gasped as a painful contraction hit her.

Oh'Dar thought but did not say aloud, *Good wolf, Kweeuu. Good wolf; protect Tehya.*

Inhrah watched as Haan and the others headed for Kthama. Kweeuu trailed happily behind, oblivious to the drama, and relieved to be back with his beloved Tehya.

Instead of going himself, Acaraho decided to stay with Tehya and sent the guard up ahead to let Khon'Tor and Adia know they were following. *I will take no chance of her not getting safely back to Kthama,* he thought. *I feel responsible for this happening in the first place since my guard could not protect her.*

They made their way to Kthama and arrived to find Adia, Nadiwani, Urilla Wuti, and Awan waiting for them.

Adia clasped her hands to her face with joy at seeing Tehya in Haan's arms, her gaze going straight to Tehya's belly. *Thank the Great Mother; she has not had the offspring.*

"Where is Khon'Tor?" shouted Acaraho as they approached.

"We do not know. No one has seen him since morning," shouted the First Guard.

Adia had a sinking feeling in the pit of her stomach. *Oh no.*

"Take me to him," said Tehya.

"Tehya, your water cradle broke. You need to go inside," said Oh'Dar.

"You need care," agreed Adia. "Haan, thank you. Please bring her inside."

"I said no! Take me to Khon'Tor!" Tehya raised her voice, sitting up in Haan's arms. "I need to see him. He needs to know I am alright. I am not asking you, I *am telling you*!" she was nearly hysterical but clearly calling on her position as the Leader's mate.

"We do not know where he is," said Awan.

"I do," said Adia suddenly. *And it is not good.*

"How do you know?" asked Nadiwani.

"I can see it. I know where he is, or where he is headed. Come on, we must hurry," and Adia took off, leading the group behind her.

Partway up, Haan turned to Hakani. "Perhaps you should not come. Whatever is going on, your presence will just inflame the situation. It was obvious when we last went to Kthama that Khon'Tor did not want you there. Wait here until I come back."

Hakani knew what Haan was saying, that her presence would only cause trouble.

She paused and let them continue without her.

☾

Khon'Tor was finally at his destination. He had made up his mind. His life was nothing without Tehya, and he knew the only way to save her was in his hands.

The debt for my crimes was never paid by the one who owed it. If I pay for what I did, perhaps Tehya will be spared. And our offspring. At least Tehya will still have some part of me.

Khon'Tor took his place a few feet from where Hakani had stepped off the path to the waters of the Great River below. Except that where she had survived, he would make sure that he did not. There was a sharp-edged blade in his left hand. The Waschini knife Oh'Dar had brought him.

Forgive me, Tehya. I have no right to happiness; I am just sorry that you became involved in this. I wish I could explain, for you must not blame yourself.

Khon'Tor squeezed his eyes shut. *I hope all of you will understand why I did this, that I am doing this to set things right. My death will pay the debt I owe—to all of you and the Great Spirit. I wish I could have seen our offspring, held her at least once. I wish I could have shared the rest of my life with you, Tehya. But in a way, I will have. It was just not enough—though no amount of time with you could ever be enough.*

Khon'Tor took another step closer to the edge and raised the blade to his throat. *Goodbye, Saraste'.*

"Khon'Tor!"

He paused, hearing what he had thought to be Tehya's voice.

"Khon'Tor, please! What are you doing? I am

here." She immediately knew what he was planning on doing. "*Stop!*" she cried out from Haan's arms.

"Put me down—please, Haan!"

Haan lowered her to the ground, but she slumped down, one hand on her belly. Adia ran to her side. "Adoeete, I am here," continued Tehya. "Come to me, please,"

"Khon'Tor," said Acaraho. "*What are you doing*?"

"What I should have done a long time ago."

"Killing yourself is not the answer. Look, Tehya is here, she is safe. Your offspring has not yet been born. They are safe and well. What you are doing serves no purpose."

"She is only alive because I promised to pay the debt I owed in exchange for her safety. And the offspring's."

"Promised *who*?" asked Adia, looking up from where she knelt next to Tehya.

"The Great Spirit. I never paid for my crimes, but you—you who are all innocent—you have suffered for my sins, not me. It was my debt to pay, never yours. It is time to make it right."

He believes this, by the Mother, thought Adia. She stood and stepped forward.

"Khon'Tor, you are wrong. You are very wrong. The One does not demand sacrifice. You are mistaken. Your grief and worry have distorted your thinking. Tehya is here. She loves you. You have a life together. I beg you, do not throw it away."

"Adoeete, please," Tehya screamed, reaching out

for him with her free hand. "Please, do not leave me!" And she clawed at the ground as she tried to drag herself to him.

"This is not good for your mate *or* your offspring, Khon'Tor," Nadiwani called out, crouching down to Tehya, trying another approach to reach him. "*You need to come away from there to her side. She needs you.*"

"The only thing any of you need from me is that I settle the debts I owe from long ago. Thank you all for believing in me, for giving me a second chance. It was more than I deserve." Turning to address Acaraho, he continued, "It has been an honor to serve with you, Commander. Take care of Tehya for me, and our offspring," he said and walked toward the edge. When he reached it, he returned the blade to his neck, and looking at Tehya, he said, "Forgive me, Saraste'. I never deserved you. Know that this time with you has been the happiest of my life, happier than I could ever have dreamed."

Adia was praying for intervention, for the words, for some way to reach him, tears streaming down her face. *Please, Great Mother*, let someone's words help him!

A trickle of bright red blood started down from where Khon'Tor was pressing the blade to his neck.

"Khon'Tor, *wait!*" shouted a voice from behind. Hakani, defying Haan's order to stay behind, stepped to the front.

Khon'Tor paused, the blade still at his throat. He locked his eyes on hers.

"What are you doing here? Have you come to gloat?" he sneered. "Well, you were almost too late. Congratulations, Hakani; you have won after all. Just as you always wanted."

"I am not here to gloat, Khon'Tor. I am here to make my own amends," she said.

"What kind of trickery is this, Hakani? Will you never tire of torturing me? This will be your last chance, so make it good. I am all ears," he said bitterly, slightly lowering the blade.

"I do not blame you for not trusting me. You have no reason to. But I hope you will at least listen. You must not do this, Khon'Tor. Your friends and your family need you. And the People need you. And not just the People of Kthama, but all the People in every community. The People are facing trying times, unprecedented times. They look up to you and trust in your strength. If you destroy yourself, how will they find the strength to face their own troubles? If the struggles of life defeat a *Legend*, as they believe you to be, where is their hope?"

Hakani hesitated just a brief moment before continuing, "It was my insecurities that started our problems. I hated you for a rejection I imagined, and I set out to punish you for it, in any way I could. Even my being seeded the first time was a lie—I mated with no other. I was never seeded with another male's offspring. I only told you that to hurt you."

Khon'Tor frowned at hearing the truth. "I suffered all these years over that, Hakani, looking at each of the males and wondering, *is this who betrayed me?*" he said quietly.

"It was just another way to torture you, to try to destroy you. *Everything* I did was designed to break you."

She saw she had his attention and so continued, "I called you a monster, but I am the monster. If it had not been for my torturing you, constantly trying to find ways to undermine you, defy you, doing everything I knew you hated, none of what you did would have happened. I truly believe this. No, I *know* it."

She paused a moment, taking her eyes off Khon'Tor just long enough to glance at Haan, then back to Khon'Tor.

"I never loved you, Khon'Tor. I only wanted the power and importance that came from being the Leader's mate. You deserved a real partner, and you did not deserve my hatred of you. There is something wrong with me that I cannot overcome. Sometimes I can see it, but then the darkness returns. But I see it more clearly now than I ever have. And whatever this distortion is, I have passed it onto Akar. You still have a chance at happiness. This one loves you," she said as she motioned back toward Tehya. "And you love her. Do not throw it away. I see it so clearly now—what I did to you, what I did to everyone. And with Oh'Dar, the High Council, anything to make trouble for Adia. Remember that, standing in this same spot, I intended to kill Nootau. If Adia had not

246 | LEIGH ROBERTS

tackled me, I would have taken him over the cliff. I was not bluffing; I wanted to hurt all of you, striking out from the tortured krell of my own soul."

She took a step closer. Khon'Tor kept his eyes locked on her but did not move.

"There is nothing for me here any longer. Akar'Tor hates me; my life at Kthama is ended. And I will not allow myself to destroy Kalli as I did Akar, ruining her life too. If there is a debt to be paid, it is mine and not yours. Do not add to my sins by taking your own life. Do not add to the damage I have already done by hurting those who love and need you."

She motioned to the others.

"These people have forgiven you. Adia set you free when she revoked her accusations against you at the High Council meeting. The leadership of Kthama is now what it should always have been— there is peace and unity now. I could have been part of that, but instead, I chose to focus my life on fighting you on every front. I never gave you a chance to be a good mate to me. Instead, almost right from the start, I was cold and rejecting. I poisoned whatever could have been between us. The debt owed is mine, not yours. Do not throw your life away. I hope someday you can forgive me. Let this nightmare end, here and now."

She turned to Haan, her voice softer, "Thank you for giving me a chance at happiness. I love you. Haaka will help you raise Kalli; she loves Kalli and will be good to her. Forgive me. I cannot—" and before anyone realized what she was doing, Hakani raced forward and ran straight off the edge to the Great River below.

The ground shook as Haan ran to the path's edge. After looking down, he fell to his knees. Khon'Tor stepped back in shock. Nobody moved, stunned, and then a moment later, Tehya screamed out in pain, snapping everyone out of their frozen state.

"This offspring is coming *now*!" yelled Adia amid all the chaos.

Tehya let out another scream as she contorted in pain. She reached out to Khon'Tor again, "Khon'Tor, pleeease," she cried, her hand outstretched.

"Khon'Tor. By the Mother, let the past die with Hakani. Choose your future. Choose to *be here for your mate*!" ordered Acaraho.

Khon'Tor released the blade in his hand, and it clinked to the ground. They all breathed a sigh of relief. Then he came away from the edge to Tehya's side.

Acaraho's guard rushed over and looked down. This time, Hakani's crumpled body was lying in plain sight at the edge of the receded waters. This time, there was no way she had survived. He looked at Haan and slowly shook his head *no*.

In the meantime, Adia and Nadiwani were tending to Tehya.

"What can I do to help?" asked Khon'Tor. Tehya

reached out and grabbed his arm, tears streaming down her face.

"Here, come around behind her, pull her onto you, and support her back."

They helped arrange Tehya in a better position, crouched against her mate, cradled between his muscular thighs.

"I have never seen it progress this fast. Especially the first time. They are both stressed. Too stressed. This offspring needs to be born *now*," said Adia. Nadiwani looked up at the Healer and said, "I do not know how, but it is time. Perhaps she has been in labor for a while already."

Adia looked Tehya squarely in the eye. "Push, Tehya. You must push with all your might," she said. "Bear down."

Tehya let out another long yell that pierced Khon'Tor's heart and pushed as hard as she could. She arched her back, her face contorted. Her nails dug deep into each of Khon'Tor's thighs, breaking the skin. A trickle of blood ran down his legs, but he bore the pain without flinching, praying for his mate and their daughter.

Oh'Dar stripped off his top wrapping and handed it to Nadiwani just as the tiny offspring was born. Everyone was immediately filled with relief.

Nadiwani quickly wrapped Oh'Dar's tunic around the tiny offspring and laid her on her mother's chest.

Tehya's arms immediately went around the little

bundle, clutching it protectively and looking back up at Khon'Tor. "She is perfect. What will we name her?" Tears of happiness were streaming down her face.

Adia was relieved to see Tehya and Khon'Tor connecting as he returned from the place of self-destruction he had been in when they found him. She turned her attention back to the offspring, and her face went blank.

"Something is wrong," Adia said. "*She has stopped breathing.*"

Tehya looked up at Adia, and realizing what she said was true, sobbed openly, Khon'Tor reached around and pulled her farther onto his lap, the offspring still cradled in her arms.

"She is not breathing!" sobbed Tehya. Adia and Urilla Wuti looked at each other. *This cannot be happening.*

Oh'Dar pushed his way forward. "Here. Let me have her!" he commanded.

He took the still, little form from Tehya and cradled her in his arms, dragging the umbilical cord with him. He stuck his little finger in her mouth, swirled it around and pulled it out, but nothing came with it. He then covered her mouth and nose with his own. The Healers looked on in confusion as they all inwardly prayed for the Great Mother's mercy.

Oh'Dar made a tiny puff, then put his ear to her nose and mouth. Nothing. Then he made another tiny puff, again covering her mouth and nose at the same time. Still no change. One more. Finally, the tiny offspring gasped, her little chest rising, and started breathing on her own again.

Khon'Tor practically collapsed with relief. Tehya cried harder, this time with tears of joy. The others all heaved heavy sighs.

"She will be alright now," he said, returning the tiny bundle to her mother's arms.

Just as had the bolt of dread passed through Adia several weeks before, a divine sense of peace now filled her. *This is why Oh'Dar had to come back. To find Tehya, and to save her offspring. Great Mother, help me never to doubt your leading again.*

Bringing herself back to the moment, Adia asked, "How did you know? How did you know to do that?" asked Adia.

"Something I learned from the Waschini. Let us all get back inside and get Tehya and the offspring settled with Khon'Tor in their quarters," he said.

As Khon'Tor gently scooped up Tehya and their daughter, Adia went over to tend to Haan, who was still kneeling crumpled on the ground where he had dropped.

"I am so sorry, Haan. I know you loved her. And I know she loved you too. She was a tortured soul who could not find peace." She placed a hand on the Sarnonn's arm as he knelt in the dirt.

"I know. But it does not make it any easier. Her hatred of Khon'Tor was unnatural. It was more than normal resentment. I suspected for some time that her mind was not right. And Akar seems to be the same, perhaps worse. I do not know if something in her blood was passed on to Akar, or if it happened as she said—because he was conceived in hatred. We will never know. But I have a daughter to take care of, and Akar to deal with, and all the problems facing my people. I will have to set this aside as best I can for now, and deal with it later."

"Is there someone to care for Hakani's offspring, your daughter?"

"Yes. Hakani's friend Haaka, she has been helping with Kalli all along. She is part of our pod, and she will be sad to hear of this." He paused. "I wonder if Hakani was thinking of this for some time? Not too long ago, she told me that Haaka favored me and loves Kalli. I wonder if she somehow knew she would not be here much longer? I will never know."

Acaraho came over to join them briefly, keeping one eye on the others, making sure Khon'Tor was safely on his way back to Kthama with Tehya. "Is there anything we can do, Haan? And, I am sorry to ask, but what would you like us to do with —Hakani?"

"Give me a few moments, and I will get her. I will take her home with me. I can find my way down to the river bank," he said.

He paused before continuing. "We still have preparations to make, for the opening of Kthama Minor. I was just waiting for a sign."

Adia did not ask if he meant this was the sign; she just silently stayed next to him.

Haan heaved himself up from his position, the weight of his grief showing in his slow movements. Adia and Acaraho watched him leave before going to catch up with the others who were making their way back to Kthama.

CHAPTER 12

Haan picked his way down to the river's edge to where Hakani lay in a heap. He knelt down by her and talked out loud to her, "I am sorry, my mate. I knew you were unhappy, tortured even, but I never thought it would come to this. In returning to Kthama to save Akar and Kalli, we re-awakened the twisted, suffering part of your soul, tearing open the wounds that never truly healed. I will take care of our daughter and make sure she knows how much you loved her. I hope you have now found the peace that you were never able to find on this side."

He gently picked up her crushed body and started a slow trek back to Kthama.

As he approached Kayerm, he was relieved to see some of his own followers outside. They ran over to him, seeing him carrying Hakani, her body splayed in an unnatural position.

"Adik'Tar, what is wrong?"

"Hakani is dead. Did Artadel return with my son? Where is Akar? I do not want him to see his mother like this," said Haan.

"Artadel did return but said that when they got back, Akar'Tor was gone."

"Gone? In the condition he was in, I do not see how."

"Nevertheless, he was. He was not in the cave, so they searched the area, and he was nowhere to be found."

Haan said, "Go and fetch Artadel, we need to make preparations for her final journey. And also, find Haaka; she must know before she hears it from someone else. They were close."

They returned shortly with Artadel and Haaka. At seeing Hakani's limp form in Haan's arms, Haaka immediately knew that she was gone. She rushed to her friend, still cradled by Haan, and hugged her anyway.

"Hakani, oh, Hakani," she said, stroking her friend's hair. "What happened?" She looked up at Haan with tears in her eyes.

"It was her choice. We knew she was troubled. We can talk about it later; is Kalli alright?"

Haaka slowly nodded. "She will never know how much her mother loved her."

"Yes, she will. I will make sure of it," corrected Haan.

They left to take care of Hakani, but on top of

everything else, Haan's mind was troubled about what could have happened to Akar'Tor.

Haan stood next to his followers and Haaka, who was holding Kalli, as Artadel conducted the burial ritual, and they said their final goodbyes to Hakani.

"I loved you. I know you loved me. At least I have some part of you with me here, in our offling. Though I failed to protect you, I promise I will protect her. Forgive me for not realizing in time how deeply troubled you were, how much your mind was in anguish. How tortured does one's soul have to be, that choosing one's own death over life is the better choice? I will never know the answer."

He placed his hand on her heart, her chest cold and still underneath his touch.

"Safe passage, until we meet again," Haan choked out the few words he could.

Tears streamed down Haaka's face as he spoke, and she clutched Kalli closer to her, rocking her gently.

Haaka spoke last, "I am sorry, my friend, that our paths have separated so early. And so suddenly. I am sorry that I, too, did not realize how tortured you were. I will never forget you. And I will do all I can to help your family. I promise."

When it was over, Artadel solemnly completed the ritual, and the males stood watch until the funeral fires died down before burying what was left of her worldly vessel. Off to the side, Haan noticed Taynor, who stood with a cruel smile on his face.

Haan and Haaka solemnly made the walk back to Kayerm. Once inside, Haaka paused to speak with Haan for a moment.

"I know this is a terrible time, but the question has to be asked. What will you do with Kalli now? Who will care for her?"

Haan looked at Haaka, remembering that Hakani had said she favored him. *It is too soon for any of that, but Hakani said Haaka loves Kalli—and the offling is used to her.*

"I was hoping you would help me with Kalli, Haaka, but perhaps it is too much to ask."

"I would be glad to, Haan. I have no mate and no offling of my own. And I have grown to love Kalli. I cannot help it; she is a happy little thing," Haaka said, looking down lovingly at the offspring in her arms.

"I am glad to hear that." *I wonder if Hakani would have said Akar was a happy youngster?* A disturbing thought about Kalli flashed through the far reaches of his mind, and he pushed it away. *No, she is half mine. Kalli will be fine.*

"Before you decide, Haaka, I should tell you that I do not know what will become of me and my following. We are committed to helping the Akassa. How do you feel about this?"

"I stand with you. I am one of the females counted to come with you. But now, with Kalli to look after, I do not believe I can be part of the preparation or Kthama Minor's opening."

"No. Someone needs to take care of her, protect her. We will figure it out. Thank you, Haaka," and he turned away.

Haaka could see he was struggling. "I will take Kalli back to my living space if you do not mind. Please let me know what you would like me to do about bringing her to you; I am not sure how frequently or when to come."

Haan nodded, not saying a word. Not trusting his voice, he signed to her, "Keep Kalli with you for the time being. I will come and find you tomorrow if that is acceptable."

In the community, there was a great deal of talk about the crime Akar'Tor had committed, which had led to this tragedy. That he had kidnapped the mate of the Akassa's Adik'Tar when she was full with offling. And now, Haan, their Leader, was left with an offling to raise, one who was half Sassen and half Akassa.

Khon'Tor, Tehya, and their daughter were settled back in their Quarters. The Leader, waiting to join them on the sleeping mat, was watching while the Healers fussed over the mother and her new offspring. Kweeuu stood in the background, awaiting permission to go to his precious Tehya.

"Alright. Have I answered all your questions?" Adia asked.

Tehya nodded yes, her daughter nestled in her arms.

"We will be back later to check, but you may send for us anytime. I do not want you worrying. Despite her rocky start, she appears to be a fine, healthy offspring. She is beautiful, Tehya. She looks very much like you!"

The young mother moved the covering away from her tiny offspring's face and agreed. She did have very light coloring. So far, she had not fussed much at all, and Tehya hoped she would be a happy soul and that her path would be smooth.

"Should she not be nursing yet?" she asked.

"She will. I will stay with you if you like, just in case," said Nadiwani, seeing that Adia was exhausted. "I will sit at the work counter; you will not even know I am here. We will give her a little time and then see if she will nurse."

Tehya looked worried.

"I am sure she will; do not be concerned. She looks perfectly healthy, and there is no reason she would not," Nadiwani added, making a mental note to choose her words more carefully.

Adia looked at Khon'Tor for his permission to

leave. He raised his hand and nodded, and Adia and Acaraho left together.

Khon'Tor took his place next to Tehya, who was leaning back against the rock wall for support.

He put his arm around her.

"I was so scared, Khon'Tor. How could you think of leaving me? I could not bear to live without you. Please, please promise me you will never think like that again. If you could feel how much I love you—" she said, choking on the words.

"I am sorry, Tehya. I will never leave you again, at least not of my own choice."

She sighed. "Look what you made, Khon'Tor! She is beautiful."

"She looks just like you. And to be fair, you helped a bit."

Tehya was glad to hear some of his humor returning.

The tiny offspring stirred and opened her eyes, looking up at her mother.

"Oh," said Tehya. "Her eyes are so light. Almost golden—how can that be?"

Nadiwani said, "What is it?"

"I would have expected her eyes to be darker, a shade somewhere between my eyes and Khon'Tor's," Tehya remarked, moving a stray hair away from the little one's face.

"I do not know how it all works. But she is beautiful, regardless," remarked Nadiwani.

"She is perfect. I will have to fight off all the males to protect her," said Khon'Tor.

Tehya chuckled and raised her hand up to caress the side of his face.

Her touch stirred his heart. *What was I thinking? How could I think of leaving her alone? She needs me. And I need her. And now, so does this little one. May the Great Spirit help whoever threatens either of them, ever again.*

"Since she is awake, see if she will latch on," Nadiwani suggested.

Tehya repositioned the tiny bundle, and they all smiled profusely when, with a little help, she began to nurse.

Nadiwani let out a happy sigh, reassured that everything was finally going as it should.

Adia and Acaraho arrived back at his quarters. Though it was not even twilight, they plopped down unceremoniously on their large fluffy sleeping mat.

She rolled over to cuddle up to him, and he protectively wrapped his arms around her.

"Are you tired?" she asked.

"Exhausted. You must be too."

Adia wanted to ask him about Lifrin, and her brother, Tar. She wanted to tell him she was seeded —and that he was going to have a son. But with the turmoil of the day, and Hakani's taking her own life, it did not seem the time.

"Then, let us get some sleep," she said and snuggled closer.

Before daylight, they awoke together. Not ready to rise, they cuddled a while.

"Acaraho? I have some good news."

"Yes, Saraste'."

"I am seeded, my love. And we are going to have a son."

Acaraho raised himself on his elbows, taking Adia with him.

"How do you know? I mean, how do you know it is a male?"

"If you lie back down and promise not to fall asleep, I will tell you," she chuckled.

"I promise you; there is no chance that I could go back to sleep. This is great news, Saraste'," he said, remembering their recent focus on making love, not on making offspring, and wondering if that was what had done it.

"Alright. You know that Urilla Wuti has advanced Healer abilities and has been teaching me?"

"Yes, I do. I remember the Connection you made with me, and of course, I remember when we used to mate in the Dream World. Before all this became real," he smiled.

"Haan said that the previous Healer was supposed to tell me how to prepare, should Kthama Minor ever be opened. And of course, she died before I came and the knowledge was lost with her. Well, we contacted her."

"What?" Acaraho wasn't sure he had heard her right. "How could you contact her? She passed decades ago. Do not tell me—"

"Yes. Here is the most amazing part. Everything we believe about how we do not die when our body does—is true. We do go on. And we are just as we are now, only better. More alive, more vibrant. I cannot explain it, but I know it to be true. Well, in the Circle of Council meeting, as Khon'Tor named it, when Oh'Dar joked that all we needed to do was go back in time and ask her, it gave Urilla Wuti the idea that we might be able to do just that. We failed the first two times we tried. We did not have enough of a Connection to her to be able to find her. So we went to visit Tar, the little brother she left behind when she sacrificed herself for you and Khon'Tor."

"So, you know the story now."

"I know part of it, but if you would tell me sometime, since you were there, I would like to hear it in your words.

"Tar is sad. Despite all these years, he seems very alone. Before we parted, she asked us to look after him, see if we could get him to take a mate."

"This is hard to take in. I believe you, of course— I am just struggling to keep up. Still trying to wrap my mind around your having talked to someone who has been gone all this time."

"She told us how to prepare. She told me I was seeded and that it is a male. I did not know myself; it is too early. But she said I needed to know enough to prepare properly before Kthama Minor is opened."

"Will this preparation—whatever it is—will it really keep you safe? And our offspring?"

"Lifrin said it would. And she said leaving Kthama would not help—I asked about that. Physical distance will not make a difference. So tomorrow, Urilla Wuti, Nadiwani, and I will start preparing. All those of us who have higher seventh sense abilities."

Acaraho lay thinking. *We are having an offspring. A son. I will have a son.* "Whatever this preparation is, you must follow the directions perfectly. Take no chances, Adia. I cannot live without you."

"I promise." Adia sighed and asked, "Do you think Khon'Tor will be alright now? This was one of the worst days of my life, truly."

"I believe he will. But we will watch him regardless."

"How did Oh'Dar know how to save Tehya's offspring? I must ask him about how he knew to do that and find out exactly how it is done."

"He will be glad to tell you, I am sure. He just did not want to talk about it right then."

"I am thinking about what Lifrin said. If I would not have known I was seeded by the time Kthama

Minor is opened—then the opening must be happening within the next couple of months."

They lay quietly together for a while.

"I need to let the others know that Tehya is back safe, and so is her offspring, though I am sure the word is spreading like wildfire already," commented Acaraho. "And I must tell them that Khon'Tor will hold an assembly as soon as they are all up to it. What are your plans for Tar, Adia?"

"I thought I would invite him to our meal table. It might help him enter the community properly if he has someone helping him along. He is too young to live like this. If we can help him in any way, it would be like thanking Lifrin for her sacrifice. Will you tell me the whole story sometime, Acaraho?"

"Yes. I will. But not right now. Right now, I want only to hold you and bask in the joy that you are bearing my offspring!"

Acaraho was right; the news had spread like wildfire through the community. Though the whole story had not entirely been pieced together, they knew that Akar'Tor had stolen Tehya and that the Healers, Oh'Dar, and the wolf had helped find and save her. They also knew that Hakani had died.

After he and Adia rose, Acaraho gathered Awan, Mapiya, and the other Leaders and shared as much as he felt wise.

Mapiya shook her head, so relieved to know that both Khon'Tor, his mate, and their daughter were alright. "Who does she look like?" she asked.

"She looks very much like her mother," said Adia. "Though her eyes are even lighter than Tehya's. They are golden with little brown specks. Strikingly beautiful. She is nursing fine and keeping her mother busy, as it should be."

"I wonder when Khon'Tor will make a formal announcement, and we will get to meet her?" Mapiya asked.

"Soon, I am sure," said Acaraho.

Acaraho was right; Khon'Tor knew he had to speak to the community soon. He struggled with what to tell them about Hakani.

Tehya was sitting up, nursing their offspring.

"What will we name her, Adoeete? We still have not discussed it."

"Whatever you wish. I am sure you will pick a beautiful name to suit her. She seems very content, does she not? For an offspring." Khon'Tor asked, marveling at the love between the two of them.

"I am thinking of Arismae."

Khon'Tor repeated it to himself, then nodded. "That suits her. It is beautiful. Where does it come from? Your family?"

"No, I think I just made it up." She looked at him and smiled.

"Even better, because she is an original—just like her beautiful mother."

Color came to Tehya's cheeks. "Come and sit by me, Adoeete," she asked.

Khon'Tor went to join her on the mat. Kweeuu moved over to make room for him, and he sat propped up next to his mate.

"Promise me. I need to hear it again. You will never leave me."

Khon'Tor placed a finger under her chin and raised her face to his. He leaned over and tenderly pressed his lips to hers.

"I promise. I will never leave you. Until death parts us—naturally—when our time comes."

She leaned her head on his shoulder.

"You have not told me everything about your time with Akar," he said tentatively. "But only if it does not upset you. I do not mean to bring up bad memories."

"He did not hurt me. As I said before, he hardly touched me, and he did not try to mate me—though I was afraid he would. I felt that he wanted to, but I believe he did not because I was with offspring. But, it was so cold in there, and I constantly worried about Arismae, if my stress was affecting her. We were in a cave with only a meager fire to warm us. He kept a boulder in front of the door, so I could not escape. There was so little to eat that I worried I might lose her as I did our first offspring when I was so sick and lost all that weight. He seemed deranged. He told me terrible lies about you, things he said his mother told him. I did not believe him. It was very hard, but thinking of you kept me going. I knew I could not give up—for your sake, and for hers," she said, looking down at the tiny, sleeping bundle in her arms.

As he watched them, Khon'Tor was relieved again that the young male had not mated Tehya. "I was afraid, after what I did to them—" Khon'Tor stopped himself, not finishing the sentence—that he had worried Akar'Tor might violate Tehya as his punishment for what the Leader had done to his mother and Adia.

"What you did to who?" she asked.

"It is a long story. But one I owe to you. After you hear it, you may leave me after all. And I will understand if you do," shared Khon'Tor, quietly.

"Nothing you can tell me will change how I feel about you, Adoeete. Nothing. I do not care what you have done. I know who you are, and I know the love we share is like none other," and as she said these words, there was a ring of authority and truth in them that registered with Khon'Tor.

I believe her. But my trials are not yet over, and I have to tell her, nonetheless. I just pray that she does not leave me. But not today. I will fight that battle another time. Today I will cherish our love and our family and my happiness—for as long as it lasts.

It took about a week before Khon'Tor and Tehya were ready to face the community. Tehya was feeling protective of her daughter. Khon'Tor knew that the word had already been spread, and he did not want to rush things. He waited until she brought it up.

"I think it is time that the People got to see Arismae. Do you?" she asked.

"Yes. If you are up to it, it is. For when do you wish me to call the assembly?"

"Tomorrow morning, perhaps? That will give me time to clean myself up and get ready. It seems I have been confined to this bed forever."

"Do you need Nadiwani or Adia to come and help you prepare?" he asked.

"I think I can manage. If you would hold your daughter later, I can sort things out around here. It seems that everything is tossed everywhere," she laughed.

Khon'Tor bit his tongue, having sworn that if he got her back safely, he would never mention her scattered wrappings again.

"What will you tell them—about Hakani? And Akar'Tor?"

"I do not think I will tell them anything—yet. This is a joyful moment. Let us not mar it with sadness and unpleasantness. There will always be an opportunity for that at a different time."

The next morning, Khon'Tor and Tehya entered the Great Chamber to see everyone seated well ahead of the Call to Assembly Horn. They took their place at the front. Tehya held the tiny bundle wrapped in a beautiful soft pelt. Kweeuu began to follow them to the front, but Oh'Dar called him over, and the wolf obeyed.

As they turned to face the crowd, a spontaneous cheer rose. Khon'Tor looked at Tehya and smiled, and let the sound continue for a moment before he raised his hand as the signal that he was ready to begin.

"Thank you. Thank you, everyone. Your support is appreciated more than you know. I stand before you happier than I could ever have imagined. The Great Spirit has blessed me far more than I deserve. Not only was I given a beautiful and loving mate, but we have both been blessed with a beautiful daughter. We are here to introduce you to *Arismae*."

Tehya beamed, seeing the smiles on the faces of the People—her people now. She wished her parents were here to see this, but she immediately pushed the thought away, not wanting it to dampen her joy.

"Who does she look like, Khon'Tor—you or Tehya?" someone shouted out.

"She looks nearly exactly like her beautiful mother," Khon'Tor replied.

"Thank the Great Spirit!" shouted someone else. And they all laughed, including Khon'Tor.

"Yes, I doubt I would make a very attractive female, though my mate surely does," and with a smile, he looked down at her. "Mother and daughter are doing fine. Everything is in order. We thank the

Great Spirit for her safe return, and I thank all of you personally for your care and support. And prayers. Please bear with us as we adjust to family life. That is all."

Surely there were many wanting to ask about Akar'Tor, whom they heard had taken her, but out of respect for the moment, they did not. That evening, as she had intended, Adia asked Tar to join them. She looked around the room, waiting for him to enter. She finally spotted him, standing uncomfortably at the edge of the eating area, so she stood up and signed for him to come over.

He awkwardly wound his way to their table.

"I am so glad to see you, Tar! Come and join us. I will have someone bring you some food."

Tar looked around uncomfortably. Sitting at the table were Acaraho, the High Protector, Adia the Healer, Nadiwani the Healer's Helper, and an older female whom, from their visit, he knew to be Urilla Wuti, the Healer from another community. A young male, whom Tar recognized as Adia's son, Nootau, scooted over to make room for him between himself and Adia. It wasn't until then that Tar noticed Oh'Dar, the Waschini whom the Healer had rescued and raised, sitting on the other side of Acaraho. He had always been fascinated by his straight black hair, unusual wrappings, and blue eyes.

"Thank you for asking me to join you," offered Tar. "Commander, it is good to see you."

"As it is you, Tar. You keep to yourself a great

deal, son. My mate and I, and the rest of us here, hope to change that. You are welcome at our table —always."

"That is gracious. Thank you."

"And I expect to see you here. I will order you if I must," said Acaraho, his face serious.

At the look on Tar's face, Adia broke in, "He is teasing you, Tar—but we do want you here." She was introducing everyone when Nimida came to join them.

"Oh, and this is my—" Adia caught herself, "—this is my adopted daughter, Nimida," she said, recovering just in time.

Nimida blushed. Adia had never called her that, but it made her happy to hear it.

"Nimida joined us after the last Ashwea Awhidi and became part of our family. As we hope you will too, in time," she added softly.

Nimida squeezed in at the end of the bench, next to Oh'Dar. She recognized but did not know the stranger at the table, but she had joined late, and no doubt, had missed the introduction.

One of the females from the food preparation area had seen Acaraho's hand sign and now brought a variety of items over to Tar. He thanked her as she placed them before him.

Adia looked at Tar, trying to work out his age. He had been young when Lifrin died, which was immediately before Adia came to the High Rocks. That would put him around ten years older than Oh'Dar.

Yes, he should not be alone so much, and he is an attractive male; somehow, we must bring him out of his shell and help him heal. Hopefully, one day he will ask for a pairing from the High Council.

As they sat there, Adia was relieved that things were returning to normal. Tehya and Khon'Tor were thrilled to have an offspring of their own, finally. Hakani was no longer a threat, and this time never would be again. Adia had hopes that Tar would become part of the family and also had hopes that he would one day become ready to take a mate, as repayment to Lifrin for sacrificing her life to save Acaraho and Khon'Tor.

However, Adia had yet to deal with telling Nootau and Nimida they were brother and sister, though how to do so eluded her still. She would have to disclose Khon'Tor's assault on her, as it was the only way to justify sending Nimida away.

Despite everything we have been through, all we have weathered, secrets from the past still haunt and threaten our peace and happiness.

Urilla Wuti, Nadiwani, and I must start preparation soon for the opening of Kthama Minor. I wish I knew what to expect. What will we find inside? And Oh'Dar; how long will he stay this time? We have so much to discuss yet. And when will he go to the Brothers and face Acise? I am so sorry he lost her. Will he ever be paired, have a family of his own?

Adia tried to clear her mind and focus on the present. She looked over at Acaraho and reminded herself how far they had come. And now she was carrying his offspring. Two miracles she would never have believed possible.

Thank you, Great Spirit. Thank you, the One-Who-Is-Three, for all the blessings we enjoy and for bringing us through the dark passages of life. Let us remember to use those times to appreciate when the path is smoothed before us. Let us find respite and gain strength from the times of peace to prepare us for the next struggles, which will always, eventually, come.

Deep within the silence of Kthama Minor, something waited.

PLEASE READ

Dear Readers,

You have made it through Book Seven. I am humbled by your continued interest in my writing. Hopefully there is something you are liking (or loving maybe even, she says hopefully) about the series to keep you coming back.

It takes months and months to write a book and get it through the review, editing, and publication process. The production costs to produce a book (cover design, editing) can easily run over $1K a book. This does not include marketing costs. It requires charts and tables of plot lines, character attributes, vocabulary lists, and ideas for twists and turns (which may or may not get incorporated). Countless hours go into the creation process from idea to rough draft, to final editing, proofreading and finally publication. Writing a book or a series is a labor of love in hopes of pleasing you, the reader.

All authors dream of creating the next hugely successful story. I am no different. Of course, it happens to very few; but I still get tremendous pleasure out of knowing that you enjoyed our work and were entertained by it. So, if you enjoyed this book, and the others before, I would very much appreciate your leaving a positive rating.

To leave a review on Amazon, click below. You

may have to sign into Amazon first. Then click "Write a product review".

Click to leave Amazon review

Even if you only leave a star rating and do not feel inspired to write an actual review, I would greatly appreciate it. Positive ratings on Goodreads are also appreciated! Five stars are the absolute best!

And if you know of others who might enjoy the series, please tell them about it. I have two more series planned in this line. Continued sales are what fund the books to come.

The next book in the series is Book Eight: The Wall of Records.

If you would like to be notified when the next books in this series are available, as well as the upcoming Series Two: Wrak-Wavara: The Age of Darkness, you can follow me on Amazon—or you can join the mailing list by visiting my website at:

https://leighrobertsauthor.com/contact

You are also welcome to join me on Facebook at The Etera Chronicles.

ACKNOWLEDGMENTS

My husband, who continues to support this obsession of mine to keep writing.

My brother Richard, who has never stopped believing in me.

My oldest brother Bob, who in my childhood made up stories for my brother Richard and me, and started me wondering "What If?"

And my editor Joy, who continues on this journey with me steadfastly at my side; putting up with my continual mis-use of- and abject failure to understand the correct use of lie, laid, lain,

My publishing support group, my coach RE Vance, and my author friends and family.

And not only my dogs, but all dogs everywhere—who make life on earth the closest thing to Heaven we will ever experience on this side of the veil.